PhilCaul Custoria's
425 Main St
Lake Placid
 # 12946   NY

WHAT WILL SIMON SAY?

WHAT WILL SIMON SAY?

Lila Sprague McGinnis

LOGOS INTERNATIONAL
Plainfield, New Jersey

WHAT WILL SIMON SAY?

Library of Congress Catalog Card Number: 73–89291
ISBN: 0–88270–074–X (Cloth)
0–88270–075–8 (Paper)

Chapter One

KATE STEPPED on his bare feet.

"Praise God!" he said.

"I'm sorry, the sun—"

"Never mind, girl. Have you met Jesus?"

"Not recently," she said.

Holding wallet and keys behind her back, Kate studied the boy who blocked the dormitory door. Shoulder-length dark blond hair, a clean white shirt, and wrinkled blue jeans—that was reasonably normal. A cross hung from a leather thong around his neck, an expensive silver cross with a delicate tracery of roses.

"If you will kindly move your feet," she said.

"Jesus is alive!" He raised his hands; his smile was radiant. "With Him, all things are possible."

"In that case, you can surely move your feet. Sleep it off inside," Kate suggested.

"I don't need sleep, I'm on a glorious trip with the Lord. I'm flying high on His love, girl. He's the one cat with perspective, you know that?"

"Oh, God—"

"Well sure, God's got perspective, but I don't call my father a cat."

A reluctant twinkle flickered in Kate's blue eyes, and she glanced away quickly, looked down at her short beige linen skirt, her tanned legs, her sandaled feet— "Let him rave on," she thought. "My rotten luck, to be a straight in the seventies."

"Jesus is my Savior, my brother. Jesus is King, praise God! The Spirit of our Lord can fall on you, girl!"

Kate edged away from the door.

"Isn't that the greatest news you ever heard?" His smile competed with the summer sun.

"Yes—well, excuse me, but my friend is waiting." Slipping around him, she flew down the steps. His voice followed her.

"Come out to the oval this afternoon! We'll sing and pray, and there'll be a preacher like you never heard before. Come and meet Jesus, face to face, all right?"

Kate reached the bottom step and turned, looked up. He stood with hands in the air, fingers widespread. His eyes were closed, his face lifted up—with a wild and irrational rush of anger, she knew he was praying for her.

"Why him? Ten thousand people on campus this summer, and I step on *his* feet. Why not a handsome *man*, if I have to step on someone? Instead, this idiot child." She sat in the familiar dark of Charlie's Cellar, having a farewell lunch with Beth. Roommates for two years at college, they had stayed together again the last six weeks, while each took a short course in special education.

~ 2 ~

"He prayed for me." Kate's fingers tapped the scarred oak table angrily. Beth moved the candle to one side and said an extra prayer couldn't hurt.

"From this barefoot kid?"

"And dirty too, I'll bet. Oh, well, Kate—"

"No, he wasn't dirty, I'll give him that. Except for his feet, he was clean enough. But telling me about Jesus—"

"That's logical, your father's a preacher. Pity me—" Beth's eyes sparkled in the candlelight. "My father works in a foundry, I attract foundrymen. You attract Jesus freaks."

"All things considered," Kate said, "I prefer a foundryman to some kid telling me about a cat called Jesus. Reminds me of the trouble in Bentley Falls—but I won't be there long, praise the Lord." Her left brow rose in a high arch. "If you'll pardon the expression," she said.

"It's too bad you won't be staying with your family, Kate. It could be exciting, you know? If your dad's new church is anything like St. Pete's back home, well if the Jesus freaks ever got in St. Pete's, the fur would fly." Beth paused to reflect, then added, smiling, "Only the most expensive furs, of course."

"But these aren't Jesus freaks causing the trouble in the Bentley Falls church."

"No?"

"Dad called it the charismatic renewal, whatever that means."

Beth nodded. "Tongue-speakers. Jesus people," she said. "Freaks."

Kate groaned, said, "Heaven help us all," and changed the subject to Beth's husband, who was overseas but due home in a week. One long, seven-day week, the end of eleven endless months. They did not mention David, or play the game of "remember when," recalling the days

~ 3 ~

when they were four undergraduates together, dreaming magnificent dreams.

Long after the second cup of coffee was finished, Kate reached for her purse and said it was time to go.

"I want to get there before dark," she said. "Otherwise I may never find the new house, and I hate to ask directions."

"Me, too." They paid for their lunches and walked back to the dorm where the cars were waiting.

"All packed and ready to go," Kate said. "Take care—"

"Gosh, look at that crowd." Beth stared toward the front campus. "Your barefoot buddy wasn't kidding, there must be a thousand kids out there."

"And not all kids, at that." Kate stared, too, then caught Beth's arm. "Come on—"

"Let's listen a while."

"You're an elephant child," Kate grumbled, but she was one herself, full of curiosity. She followed Beth across the street, stood by the wide trunk of a sycamore, where she could see the people. Long-haired, short-haired, barefoot, and shod. Old and young sprawled on the green grass or sat in bright aluminum chairs, listening to a man on a wooden platform, shouting at a microphone.

"When I was a little fellow, I went to church every Sunday with a lot of dead people!" He wasn't little now; he was tall, skinny, and what was left of his hair blew about his face like dried grass. "I went to church with dead people; they sat, and they stood up, and they didn't know why they were there—"

"Amen, brother!" Sounds of agreement floated through the crowd. Maybe they all go to church with dead people, Kate thought.

"They came every Sunday because their mamas had come every Sunday," he shouted. "But they didn't know how to worship the Lord. They were afraid someone would

~ 4 ~

hear them—maybe they were afraid the Lord would hear them!"

"Amen." "Praise God!"

"You know their favorite verse in the Bible?" The preacher chuckled into the mike, delighted with himself. " 'The Lord is in His Holy temple, let all the earth keep silence before Him.' Yeah, brother, that's, the way they worship."

Heads nodded agreement, and Kate's lips drew tight. Her father often used those words, spoke them in his careful, clear voice. They were good and beautiful words. This man was a moron, or worse. Irritated with the speaker, and with herself for listening, she tugged Beth's arm.

"But you want to know my favorite verse? The favorite verse of all the Jesus people everywhere?" He waved long arms in the air. "Make a joyful noise unto the Lord!"

"Hallelujah! Praise God! Bless the Lord!" Laughter and praise swept through the audience.

"They're all mad. Come on, Beth."

"Coming. But they're happy, Kate. See the smiles—"

"Most idiots are happy," Kate said.

"Hey, girl!" She turned quickly at the sound of that familiar voice, saw him weaving his way through the bodies on the ground. The silver cross gleamed in the late afternoon sun. The crowd began singing.

"Turn your eyes upon Jesus," they sang. "Look full in his wonderful face."

"Sister!" He shouted above the singers. "Wait, girl— hey!"

Kate gripped Beth's wrist and pulled her across the grass, the street—they must hurry to escape that long-legged child. She did not want to turn her eyes upon Jesus.

They reached the dorm and raced up the steps. Safely inside, they leaned against the door, laughing.

~ 5 ~

"Stupid," Beth gasped, "to run from a harmless kid."

"Maybe he's harmless. Anyhow, I didn't want to share you just now." They hugged each other fiercely. "Beth, be happy," Kate whispered. "Be happy for all four of us. Love him, love him—"

"I will. Listen, Kate, I will."

"And write to me!" Kate fled then, before the tears came. She rushed through the back hallway to the car, and through the mist found her keys, opened the lock and slid inside.

"Girl, wait." Tanned fingers on the door. Kate looked up—bright blue eyes and a silver cross.

"Tears? Hey, now—" His young face looked dismayed.

"Never mind," Kate muttered, but he was already praying—the nerve of that kid, he was praying!

"Almighty Father, bring joy to this child of yours. Wipe all her tears away."

"Dammit—"

"In the name of Christ Jesus, our Savior, and I thank You, Lord."

The motor caught, the car jerked backward and stopped. He stood with arms high, his face lifted; shadows moved across it as the wind blew the leaves overhead. He spoke in a strange mixture of sounds, no language that Kate knew, but some language certainly, then stopped speaking and dropped his hands.

"Praise the Lord," he called, laughing. Kate fastened her seatbelt and let up on the brake; the car swung around and moved out of the lot.

He stood in the street, waving—damn fool kid—until she turned the corner.

Ten minutes later she slipped onto the freeway west of town and she was singing. Hearing herself in the quiet of the car, she closed her lips quickly, then relaxed and smiled.

She was through crying, but no thanks to that freak. She'd stopped crying two and a half years before, when she knew that nothing would bring David home from Vietnam.

Those tears, as parting with Beth brought vivid memories, were forgivable, she thought, if I get myself together now.

She passed a moving van—WE'LL MOVE YOU EVERYWHERE WITH LOVING CARE—and turned the radio on. A little hard rock would stomp out thinking. A little jazz—

> Amazing grace, how sweet the sound,
> That saved a wretch like me—

"Damn it all to hell," Kate said.

Chapter Two

KATE FOUND Christ Church in Bentley Falls a little after seven that evening. It was gray stone and Gothic; a tremendous oak tree in front was almost as tall as the bell tower. Beyond it, up the side street, she could see a newer section—classrooms and offices, she supposed. The parish house. Directly behind the church was a parking lot, and Willow Street, beyond the parking lot, was their street. She turned and recognized her father's car in the drive of the first house, and her brother's familiar figure, polishing the whitewalls. Could he possibly have a date, twenty-four hours after they moved to town?

Knowing Pete as she did, she knew he could. She turned in the drive, stopped with a simultaneous push on the horn, and waved, laughing, when he leaped to his feet with an alarmed shout.

Pete opened her car door—a two-car family at last, he

told her, grinning—and she met the rest of the Thornes
halfway in the yard. The Reverend Mr. John Thorne came
first, moved fastest, and stopped to grin at her, his usual
small smile transformed into a large one. Kate stopped and
grinned back; she knew their smiles matched. She remembered a little white-haired lady saying, "My dear, you look
enough like your father to be his daughter," and she
remembered, too, the lady's charming confusion when she
realized what she'd said. They did look alike. Kate had her
father's square face and the smile that nearly closed his
eyes, although he did not have Kate's dimple in his left
cheek, and her light brown hair was not thinning on top.

"Well, Kate," he said now, and she laughed, hugged
him, hugged Margaret Thorne and kissed them both. When
a teenager, Kate had desperately wished that she looked like
her mother, but Margaret's oval face and dark brown hair
skipped Kate and went to Pete and Nora.

"Where's Nora?" Kate needn't have asked; a slight
figure came racing across the porch, and she was surrounded
by Nora. Thirteen, long legs and arms, dark hair confined to
pigtails because, she explained, she'd been working.

"Come see my room, Kate, it's the greatest, and I don't
have to share it with you!" She caught her breath and
changed that. "I mean you don't have to share with me, you
have a room all to yourself, but mine is definitely the best.
Wait until you see—it's pink."

"You get the guest room," Pete told Kate, lifting her
bags from the trunk and bringing them across the lawn.
"But be not misled, you are no guest. We have no room for
a non-worker. You wouldn't believe the junk we brought
across the state. Our parents are sentimental fools."

He disappeared into the house, and Margaret put her
arm through Kate's, drew her toward the door.

"Don't believe everything your brother says about us,

until you check his room," she said. "He used his sleeping bag last night because I couldn't get close enough to his bed to put sheets on it."

Inside, Kate was given a quick tour of the downstairs. In the kitchen, the window above the sink was shaded by a middle-aged maple tree and gave a view of the church parking lot beyond the drive. The dining room had a bay facing the shaded backyard and the parish house.

"That's my office, the first window near the gap in the hedge," John told her. "Nice and close for rainy weather."

The living room was large, and blessed with a fireplace, and Pete was right. Boxes were everywhere.

Kate dropped onto the mercifully uncluttered sofa and said she was not sure the month of vacation would be enough. "Unpack all this in four weeks, mother?"

"Of course. Four days, I should think. People kept dropping in all afternoon to help."

"Which explains why the boxes are still full. How many cups of tea did you serve?"

"Thousands." Nora answered for her mother. "I know—I had to wash the cups. Now come on—" and Kate was taken to the second floor, shown the pink room and Pete's room and the guest room.

"Your room," Margaret said. "And I wish you could stay in it, I really do."

There was blue wallpaper with tiny white flowers above white wainscoting, and Grandmother Thorne's brass bed spread with a quilt her other grandmother had pieced long before from bright bits of fabric. Kate, getting ready for bed later that evening, her suitcase open on top of two boxes, wished she could stay in this delightful room, too. But the wish was fleeting; she quickly remembered the freedom of living in the city, even in a boarding house, where no one cared if you were happy or sad, no one asked where you were going or if you were going, and why not.

And, of course, where no one loved you.

She lay down, pulled the sheet up and threw it back again, suddenly aware of the August heat. She'd signed a contract, and her job was waiting. Her students in need of special tutoring and unlimited patience would come hopefully the first week in September, and she would be there, as she had been there the last year, and the year before. It was a satisfying kind of job, although difficult, and the blue and white room was perfect for guests.

But the next day, just after lunch, a sturdily built young woman with dark, square-cut bangs and a postman's hat, gave Kate a letter. A letter that had gone first to their old home and been forwarded here, postmarked Cleveland.

Sitting on the steps, she read the letter, noted the postmark was a week old, and thrust it into the pocket of her shorts. She walked slowly across the yard and stood touching the hot steel of her car, decided against driving and went on, strolled across the parking lot behind the church, frowning in the sunlight, and reached the big tree in front before she remembered she'd promised to help in the office.

The plaque on the front door said, "Enter, Rest and Pray," but the door was locked. To Kate, it seemed, somehow, logical. Walking around the church, she opened the door of her father's office. The office was empty.

Kate stepped inside, closed the door, and breathed in the air-conditioned atmosphere, stepped across a half-emptied box and dropped into the large desk chair. Nice. Whatever his failings as a pastor, if any, the late Mr. Washburn, her father's predecessor, had liked comfort. She read the letter once more and placed it firmly on the desk. She would think about it later.

Except, of course, that it was impossible to think of anything else. She swung her feet up, onto the desk, pushing a book out of the way to make room, and noticed that three different translations of the Bible lay in the middle of the boxes on the floor, all of them open at Romans. Her father had begun unpacking, been struck by a new idea or a new light on an old one, stopped to consider it, and forgotten the job at hand. Which was normal.

She closed her eyes. That letter from Mrs. Haskell must be answered, but—

"Well, Kate." Mr. Thorne stood in the doorway, wearing a short-sleeved black shirt with a clerical collar. A black suit coat drooped over his arm. "Siesta already?"

"Just gathering energy to tackle this mess," she answered, laughing, swinging her feet back to the floor. "Why the somber garments? You looked absolutely festive in that plaid shirt and those unforgivable shorts—"

"Hospital call. If I can find the hospital."

"In Bentley Falls? Come now, father."

"Forty-five thousand people, Kate, no telling where they've put the hospital. But I have a map." He dropped the jacket across a box and began to take books up, put them on the shelves. "Where'd you get to, anyhow? I called—"

"Just walking, around the church. I had a letter from Mrs. Haskell."

"Your boss?" He put volume two of *The Interpreter's Bible* back into the open box and looked at Kate.

"*Was* my boss. The government isn't renewing the grant for our school, so I'm temporarily unemployed."

"Can they do that? My word, it's the end of July."

"First week in August, in fact. And they can and they did. She's offered me another contract, a regular English assignment. I won't starve."

He lifted the heavy book again and slid it onto the shelf. "If it's a new contract, I suppose you don't have to sign it?"

She'd known he would see that, would immediately see that. "No, I don't have to take it," she said, and turned away to open another box, to sort the books. That was the decision she must make, and quickly.

Did she want to go back to Cleveland, now that she had a choice? Would she rather stay here?

Or perhaps she didn't have a choice, even now. This late in the summer, her chances of finding a job—she was certified in English and history, as well as remedial reading —were slight. Teachers weren't as scarce as they had been even two years ago. The few hours she'd earned toward her master's the last two summers were not that impressive.

But supposing she found a job—did she want to stay? Would it be helpful to her parents to have another listening ear, if the rumors they'd heard were true, if trouble did develop in Christ Church? Or would it be better if she went away?

"Kate, you might consider—" Mr. Thorne paused; she knew it was because he hated to interfere, even with a suggestion. "We—your mother and I—would welcome your staying, if you think—we'd like it very much. You do know that?"

"I know it, I do. But would I be useful? I mean—do you expect a real problem?"

"No, the Bishop was mistaken, I'm sure. Aldous—Mr. Washburn—told him about the tensions, but—"

"They don't exist, these tensions?"

"Well, we've only been in town since Saturday, Kate. It's too early to know. But I doubt it."

"No one shouted 'Praise the Lord' during Sunday service? No one gave a prophecy in Chinese? How dull."

"Wouldn't that be something?" He sat back on his heels, considering. "What would I do, I wonder?"

"You'd say 'Amen, brother,' find your place in the prayer book, and go right on, of course."

"Perhaps I would." He sat looking out the window, his slight smile announcing his pleasure with the world as well as his acknowledgment of its deficiencies. Things will look better tomorrow, his smile proclaimed, but not a lot better. "Listen, Kate, why don't you check around? They might be desperate."

"And it might snow," she said. "Of course, I could try the county schools too. I'd like that, I think, a complete change from the inner city."

"You would apply? Look into it?" He sounded wistful but his movements were suddenly quick as he stood up, brushed off his pants, slipped into his jacket. "I'd better get on. I might get lost in Bentley Falls." He went out the door, taking the path through the hedge and across the rectory yard to his car.

Bentley Falls—Kate thought how strange it was that they were here, at all. Home was St. Paul's, in a small city across the state. Yet all of a sudden, here they were.

Not, of course, all of a sudden. She'd been at home that weekend when Mr. Thorne told his family that the Bishop wanted him to move, that the committee had asked him to come. Nora was furious. Pete asked about the track team, the football team, and if he could drive, come moving day. Margaret had not exactly said, "Whither thou goest—" but her smile had said it all.

Chapter Three

KATE, SUDDENLY ANXIOUS to talk to her mother, put books away more quickly. She stacked the papers on one of the shelves near the desk and hoped her father would find time to sort them, soon.

The final box was emptied at last; Kate piled it with the others by the door and surveyed the order she had wrought. Dad would use unclerical words before he found what he wanted and organized this place, but at least it looked good. To the casual visitor it would seem a model of scholarly neatness. She closed the office door and took the path across the yard.

"Mother?" She stepped into the kitchen. "What in the world are you doing, just sitting here? Disgraceful!"

"I'm being grateful." Margaret Thorne's blue eyes smiled, seeing Kate. "I came down to start dinner, my mouth all set for chops and baked potatoes, and I found that." She waved toward the stove and a blue and white casserole. "Someone left it there."

"Someone named I. Spencer," Kate said, twisting her head to read the words written on a piece of adhesive tape, stuck to the side of the dish. "Not chops and potatoes."

"I know. I was furious with I. Spencer, until I sat down and realized how tired I was, and how hot, and thought how nice, no cooking after all. I decided to love I. Spencer, whoever she is. Besides, it smells good, and she put a salad in the refrigerator."

"I. Spencer makes herself at home, doesn't she?"

"Yes, and I'm glad." Margaret rubbed the back of her neck and told Kate to pour herself a cup of tea. Kate followed orders and settled on the chair across the table. Her mother looked tired, as well she might, Kate thought, moving on Saturday, church and a reception yesterday, and people—no, parishioners, not people—in and out all the time. "Listen, I have a problem and I need your help. I know the Bishop wanted dad here because of the possible mess—"

"Exaggerated," Margaret said. "I haven't heard the slightest whisper of trouble."

"Of course you haven't. You never listen for the undercurrents."

"Nonsense, I always listen carefully. I've met dozens of Christ Church people, and they've all been lovely."

"Precisely what I mean. They couldn't all be lovely, mother." Kate brushed short strands of brown hair from her eyes. "Some of them were stuffy, some dull, some bigots, some charming, but to you—all lovely. You didn't hear any rumors?"

"About that—that—" Margaret couldn't say it and Kate, laughing delightedly at her mother's unbelief, said it for her.

"That tongue-speaking. The charismatic renewal the Bishop is so concerned about because he thinks it will take money away from the church."

"Kate!"

"Well, he has to be a businessman, doesn't he? And if the wealthy members of Christ Church take their money and membership elsewhere, because of this odd element popping up, destroying the splendid dignity, well, that's trouble."

"It would be too bad, but you know perfectly well the Bishop is not a worldly man. He's more interested in the spiritual welfare of his people than he is in their last wills and testaments. You know he is!"

"I know he is. You mustn't take everything I say so seriously." Kate thought about the Bishop a moment, remembering his large head with the thick, gray hair, and his comfortably plump body, the amazing voice that made the old cathedral windows rattle when he asked the time of day. He was a good man. But why he chose her father for Bentley Falls remained a mystery to Kate. Not that John Thorne ran away from trouble. His policy was to stand still, actually, until the trouble gave up and ran away from him. It usually did. He would listen sympathetically to the people on both sides of a quarrel, and somehow the problem would disappear.

"What I don't understand," Kate began, sipped the tea, made a face and stirred more sugar into it while she sorted her thoughts. "What I really want to know is what the Bishop wants dad to do? Drum them out of the church, these fanatics we heard about? And how do you do that?"

"I don't believe there are any fanatics in our church, dear, and if there were, neither your father nor the Bishop would drum them out—whatever you mean by that."

"Isn't that what Mr. Washburn wanted to do? Before he killed himself?"

"He didn't kill himself, Kate. He lost control of the car and hit a tree."

"Precisely." Kate nodded. It was exactly what she meant—driving by yourself at high speed and hitting a tree is as quick and efficient a way of suicide as any other. However—

"I don't believe he did it on purpose," Margaret said. "He was always a nervous man. John says he may have been troubled about the state of the church furnace as easily as the state of his people. And he missed a curve."

"Call it the furnace, then. But we know he saw the Bishop and asked how to handle them, those people who were getting too religious. And the Bishop dumped the problem on dad. So what I'm wondering—" Kate pushed the letter from Mrs. Haskell across the table and finished her tea while Margaret read it.

"Oh, Kate . . ." a long and happy sigh; she, too, saw the possibilities. "Would you look for a job around here, then? The house is big enough, you could have the east room to yourself. It would be wonderful, Kate, if you wanted—"

"But supposing I found one, would that be good or bad? Hassled by the fanatically religious on one hand, and a daughter with no religion on the other? Poor dad."

"No religion? Nonsense."

"Well, is pragmatism a religion? I believe in that casserole, because I can reach out and touch it. It's real. I believe in your loving me because you show your love, you care for me. But as for God—what has He done for me lately?"

There was a long silence before Margaret said, laughing a little, "Well, there is this letter."

"You aren't going to call the federal government God, are you? Good heavens, mama!"

"No, certainly not." Margaret smiled. "But the fact that they canceled the program for your school, and the possibility that you may stay here this year, now that's a gift."

"An accidental gift." Margaret reached for Kate's hand and held it tight, but whatever she intended to say was stopped by a knock at the back door. "Oh, dear—" Kate went to the door.

A tall man stood on the second step, holding a covered platter. Brown eyes, an attractive smile, and a thousand freckles, topped by thick red hair and long sideburns. A blue suit in this heat, without a wrinkle in it; a blazing red and orange tie. Straight from the Emerald Isle, thought Kate.

"Simon Garcia," he said, pushing the platter toward her. "My mother sent—"

"Garcia?" Kate's laughter escaped before she could stop; it was too incongruous. He sighed and shook his head reassuringly.

"My paternal grandmother was a Murphy, my mother a McLaughlin," he explained, with the patient air of one who has done it hundreds of times before. "She sent this over, said you would be tired."

"Oh—I'm sorry!" Kate flushed. "Please come in, and thank you. This is my mother, Mrs. Thorne, and I'm Kate."

"I can't come in, thanks. But welcome to Bentley Falls, Mrs. Thorne, Miss Thorne—and praise the Lord you've come. Christ Church was in great need."

He paused; Kate felt an answer was expected.

"Yes, three months is a long time without a minister," she said slowly. "Sunday services, for communion especially—"

"Oh, as to that—" Simon Garcia shrugged, as though services of worship were the least of all. "We managed, you know, with vacationing firemen and the Bishop's young men. But our flock needs a shepherd."

His smile flashed again, and he lifted his hand in salute. "Praise God," he added, turned and went down the steps. Kate watched him stride across the backyard and step long legs over the low fence, into the church parking lot, before she turned back to Margaret.

"Praise the Lord, a shepherd? What kind of talk is that?" Her left eyebrow went up, her dimple in. "Could he be one of Mr. Washburn's fanatics? A Jesus freak?"

Margaret ignored Kate's question, saying instead that he brought the gift from his mother. "Not his wife," she added thoughtfully. Kate chortled.

"Chicken," she reported, peeking under the aluminum wrap covering the platter, "and don't, please, start lining up the bachelors, or I will fly the coop. Confine your efforts to girls for Pete." The phone rang, stopping her, which was just as well since Margaret wasn't paying the least attention.

A tear-filled voice asked for Reverend Thorne.

"Mr. Thorne has been called to the hospital," Kate said, stressing the "Mister" slightly, knowing her father disliked the adjective used as a title. "May I take a message for him?"

"Yes—no—I'll call back. Yes, I'll do that. I'll call back."

"May I tell him who called?"

"This is Isobel— No, I'll tell him," the voice said. "Did you find the casserole, Mrs. Thorne? I put it on the stove. I called out, you see, but—"

Kate put two and two together quickly.

"Mrs. Spencer? This is Kate Thorne, and my mother did find the casserole, and appreciates it so much. If there is any way we can help—"

"Oh, there isn't, really. But if I could talk to Reverend —to Mr. Thorne, I could— Has he been saved, Miss Thorne?"

"My father?" Kate held the phone away, looked at it blankly. Had she heard what she thought she'd heard?

"Yes, if he's been saved—I mean—oh, dear. I'll call back." Mrs. Spencer hung up.

"Who was it, dear?"

"Mrs. Spencer of the blue and white casserole, I believe." Kate replaced the receiver. "I say, mother, has dad been saved?"

"Your father? Why Kate—only we don't call it that, we say salvation, we don't say being saved, no, really we don't. It's not a term— Kate, why are you laughing?"

"Because it's so funny, Mrs. I. Spencer asking if my saintly father was saved."

"Well, I wouldn't call him saintly, exactly."

"I wonder. He came to Bentley Falls, didn't he?" Kate perched on the kitchen stool. Bentley Falls was turning up some odd ones, even as Beth predicted. Mrs. Isobel Spencer sounded like an older sister of her barefoot beau on the campus.

She shifted on the stool and leaned against the wall. It was difficult to understand these Jesus people, just as she had never understood the rebels who began the riots on campus, who burned the buildings. But even without understanding, she envied them, because they had a cause they believed in fiercely. And she wondered, because all her meditations led to this eventually, whether if David had not taken his new degree in music and all her love to Vietnam three years ago, or if he had taken them and come home again, instead of ending three weeks later as a pile of useless rubble because of a comrade's drug-hazed carelessness, would she be envious now?

~ 21 ~

She thought not. Life with David, whose idea of living was music and laughter, whose goals soared beyond the ordinary, whose children (for by now, they might have had children) would have been blue-eyed and beloved—no, she would not be envious.

It was such an ignominious ending for her laughing musician, that casket they dared not open, the odd pieces of gear sent home, including the harmonica he'd carried in his pocket, still shining. She'd given it to him in June. It was returned in time for Christmas, the year she was a senior at the University.

However. Kate placed these thoughts back in the furthest part of her mind and shook her head. Short, brown hair flew up and settled, her wide mouth turned up in a smile—forced, perhaps, but still a smile as she watched Margaret fixing salad on small, white plates. Dwelling on that time would not solve the question of whether to stay or go back to the city. She loved the inner-city youth, both black and white, world-weary yet oddly ignorant kids. One, who lived all her life within twenty blocks of the center of Cleveland, had never been to the center, never seen the tower or the monument, the newer fountains. And she was sixteen years old. Another—but this, too, was futile. The government had settled it for this year, at least, and the school Mrs. Haskell offered was different. She felt no nagging sense of loyalty to it.

On the other hand, perhaps she was needed here, as a friendly buffer if nothing else. Her parents were such credulous people, too-good-to-be-true people.

John Thorne would snort at that, but it was true, Kate thought. They would hurt no person, and assumed that no person could hurt them. Kate knew better, and she was afraid for them. Perhaps her duty—

" 'When duty whispers low, thou must, the youth

replies—' But I'm no longer a youth, mother. Have I quite lost all my bloom?"

A gurgle of laughter escaped Margaret as she bent to check the casserole she'd put in the oven. "Not quite," she said.

Closing the door, she turned to smile at Kate. "Twenty-four is not senile, dear. You've held your looks well, I think. And it is not your duty, Kate. If you could stay, if you want to stay, it—"

"If I can find a job. That's the center, and of course it isn't my duty. But this is the third of August— Oh, well, it couldn't hurt to ask. I may have to take Mrs. Haskell's offer." But if I do, she thought, collecting silverware to put on the table, if I do, at least they will know I've tried. "Don't get your hopes up, mother."

Margaret nodded, said she wouldn't. Kate took the silver into the dining room and began to lay it on the blue placemats. She knew what her mother was thinking; she was thinking she would alert the Lord, her way of saying she would pray. What possible good this would do, Kate could not see. Either the schools had faculty to hire yet, or they didn't. If they did, she might get a job. If they didn't, she would head for Cleveland in September. The first week in August was a little late for her mother's Lord to interfere.

Kate imagined a benevolent God shifting His small people around on the board of the world, making room for one more in Bentley Falls, and she snickered, then decided that iced tea would be appropriate for this hot day, and went into the kitchen to make it.

Chapter Four

WHEN JASON BENTLEY built his mill beside Clear River in 1837, a town developed around it, as he intended it should. Thirty years later, when he tried to make Bentley Falls the county seat, he failed. That honor and glory went to a smaller town, ten miles to the south, because it was the geographical center. His mill was torn down in 1923, not a moment too soon, and a park made in its place beside the river, a small park just half a block wide and a block long. The park still gives pleasure to the people of Bentley Falls, and the county seat is still ten miles south.

Kate drove those miles and discovered the offices of the Rivers County Board of Education in a house. A large house, certainly, and the showplace of the county seat eighty years ago, but still a house. Outside, it was newly painted, even the gingerbread that still outlined the many gables. Inside, the house was twentieth century modern office: color coordinated filing cabinets, pale green walls, light oak chairs and desks, and movable partitions that were changed according to need—or someone's whim.

Following the graceful, curving stairway, with the ebony railing saved by the superintendent's secretary from the summer's freshening of green, Kate reached the superintendent's office, offered her credentials, and stated her situation clearly.

The man behind the desk—he weighed three hundred pounds at least—kept nodding as she spoke. He sat on a chair twice as wide as a normal one, and twice as strong, she hoped, and tapped the fingers of one hand against the other while he listened and finally, when she stopped, leaned forward, smiling.

"Providence, Miss Thorne," he said. "I'll admit, I was irritated when Mrs. Collins called on Friday afternoon. The last day of July, her husband is transferred to Houston, and she is going with him. I'm all for family solidarity, you understand, but when my staff was filled—"

He paused, and Kate waited. He seemed to be catching his breath more than wanting an answer.

"Of course, English teachers are not exactly rare— Now, a good vocal instructor— Do you sing, Miss Thorne?"

"No." She considered qualifying that, after all, doesn't everyone sing? Then she smiled. "No," she repeated.

"Neither do I. You'd think, with all this—" he tapped his chest lightly, a smile across his wide, fat face. "But it's a little matter of carrying a tune. Volume I can get. All the academic positions were filled as of last Thursday, a minor miracle that, and on Friday Mrs. Collins called. On Tuesday you arrive. And you teach English, and that's a good thing. I'll just call Gore and see if he's handy."

"Where would it be?"

"Ford Township School, consolidated, northern part of

~ 25 ~

the county, about six, seven miles from your front door. You wouldn't have a transportation problem? Good." He rolled his chair toward the telephone; his arms were too short to reach the width of the desk. Kate listened while he exchanged a few words about the rain, or rather the lack of it, being bad for the corn, and then told the person on the line about the possible new English teacher.

Ten minutes later she drove away from the county seat, on a road slightly west of the road to Bentley Falls, toward Ford Township School. She was to meet a man called Alexander Gore. The superintendent had risen to his feet when she left. He was not at all light on his feet, but lumbered across the room to bid her goodbye, to thank her for coming in answer to their need.

"Providence, Miss Thorne," he muttered again, as she went out.

But it wasn't, of course, providence. The vacancy had come on Friday, before Mrs. Haskell's letter, before her mother alerted the Lord. It was simply the off-chance. If this Alexander Gore approved of her, and if she wanted to stay after meeting him and seeing the school—

Alexander Gore, who grows corn. Or if he doesn't grow corn, is concerned about those who do. Kate turned at the corner by the Gulf station, as she had been told to do, and decided to concentrate on the countryside. She had supposed a man named Campbell would be a spare, sandy Scotch type, and instead, the superintendent was built like Humpty Dumpty. And Simon Garcia, with his red hair, who brought fried chicken to back doors, praised the Lord in a voice that just missed having a brogue. Better to study the new land than to imagine what an Alexander Gore might look like.

The farm buildings looked prosperous, the occasional strips of houses along the road well cared for. Cows, red and white, jerseys, maybe? or guernsey? Or were they the same? Kate grinned at her own ignorance and thought that if she taught in the country, she might just learn a thing or two.

Horses! Kate resisted the temptation to pull over, beyond the sign that said "Stafford's Stables." Along with every other ten-year-old, she'd dreamed of owning a horse of her own, and the dream died slowly. She turned her head for a last glimpse of three splendid horses—at least, they seemed splendid—but she kept on, down the highway.

Past the church on the next corner, a community church, it said, although what community Kate couldn't imagine, since there was no house in sight except a gray shingle one in the trees by the churchyard. Over a rise, turn right at the next corner, and she saw the school.

The center section was two stories high, and from that, low, obviously new, wings spread out. At the far end, a gymnasium, from the shape of it. Apparently the school board in Rivers County hadn't heard that land was scarce and should be used sparingly.

A small, gray Volkswagen scooted into the drive ahead of her, from the opposite direction, and stopped in front of the center door. Kate followed, drew up beside it, and watched the man getting out.

Not tall, five ten, maybe, thin and tanned, dressed in a short-sleeved blue shirt, dark pants and clean white sneakers, he came quickly to her door, and helped her out of the car as she finished her inventory. Dark curly hair brushed back, blue eyes, and a mole that disappeared as he smiled.

"Miss Kathryn Thorne?"

"Kate Thorne," she said. "Yes."

"I'm Alex Gore." The small, brown mole at the corner of his left eye appeared for a second and was hidden again as he told her that she was more welcome than a good rain, and that's very welcome, indeed. They walked into the building, Kate took a deep breath, and he laughed.

"Fantastic, isn't it? That smell? Every room in the place was painted this summer, and still it smells like a school, you couldn't mistake it."

"I like it," she said, and he nodded. Obviously, he liked it, too.

They inspected the room she would have, on the second floor of the old building. Three freshman English classes, he said, and two junior ones. Lunchroom duty every few weeks, lunches served at school not too bad, actually, but the majority of students brought their own. As did the majority of the faculty. Probably one study hall every day and one other to be shared, maybe end up two, three days a week. One free period each day, hopefully. All the teachers supposed to stay until the last bus left, although they didn't always stay. Teachers required to arrive by eight o'clock, half an hour before school begins. Early buses unload about a quarter to eight, but the kids stay in the cafeteria then, until eight-fifteen. Or outside if the weather is nice, and if they prefer.

"Your homeroom will be juniors, I think, from L to S probably, although I've not finished with the scheduling yet. A computer would be finished by now, but we don't have the use of a computer yet. One day. Pass another levy."

He did not seem concerned about the levy. Probably has a mathematical mind, she thought, and laying out schedules for four grades of kids in heaven knows how many courses for eight periods a day, seeing that no class is too large or too small, no student ends up in a class he shouldn't take, all that doesn't bother him. A challenge, no doubt, for a rainy summer day or two.

"Takes weeks," he said, and she laughed because he'd

caught her thoughts, although it occurred to her immediately that this might be an uncomfortable trait in a principal, someday. "Of course, there's a pattern, but then you add a new course, or forty more kids, and whammo—so much for the pattern. But I keep thinking, that computer, some day . . ."

They walked back to the office, footsteps echoing in the empty building. Almost empty. Kate asked about the odd sound and was told they were doing the gym floor that week, getting ready for the autumn assault.

"Nan ordered me to bring you home for lunch, so I hope you'll come. It isn't far. A form of bribery, of course, but minor."

Kate laughed and agreed to come for lunch. In the city, one seldom met the wives of the faculty, but apparently the country would be different. They walked out into the sunshine, and she noticed how he looked up, quickly—hoping, she supposed, for rain clouds. There were none. He was attractive, this Alexander Gore. Not precisely handsome, but close enough; what had the superintendent called him? Sound. Well, he did seem to be sound, if that meant knowledgeable about his work, articulate, enthusiastic. And agile, too, she thought, as he reached her car first and opened the door for her. Their eyes met for a moment, they smiled, and Kate said something she had not intended to say.

"I never met an Alexander before," she said, realized the remark was too personal and wished it back. He laughed.

"Neither have I, but at that I'm lucky," he said. "My mother considered Gore an ugly name, and to make up for it she wanted us to have beautiful given ones—she nearly called me Bartholomew."

"What made her change her mind?"

"She read that Alexander meant 'protector of men,' and

she was a hopeless romantic. Not that it makes much difference around here," he added reflectively. "With a name like Gore, you can imagine what they call me."

"The kids, you mean—oh!" She laughed.

"You're right. Anything from Bloody Alexander on down. Bloody for short." He laughed again and told her to follow his car.

They went half a mile north of the school, turned at the corner—Parsons Road, the sign said—and the gray bug darted into a drive shaded by two horse chestnut trees. Kate followed more sedately and parked, looked out at a small green house. No barns, couldn't be a real farmer, but there were three assorted sheds, all painted the same gray-green. She was looking at the house again, admiring, when he opened the car door.

"I wanted to paint it white with red trim," he said, "but Nan figured the green would blend it into the hillside, and show off her daffodils. Would you believe a million bulbs? Come around next May and see."

"If you really mean a million, I'll be here. And I like the green paint."

"You'd better; otherwise, your chances of a good lunch are considerably less." He turned and waved at the girl coming across the lawn, a slim girl in dark shorts and a white blouse, looking as fresh as the green paint. Her dark hair reached below her shoulders, her eyes were the same bright blue as his, and her smile—

"Miss Kate Thorne, my sister, Nancy Gore," he said, and Kate thought, "Of course." Good heavens, they were just alike except that the curls and the height went to Alex.

"I'm truly glad to meet you," Nancy said, holding out her hand to Kate. "Of course you know you're the answer to our prayers?"

Kate tensed. Surely this pretty girl wasn't one of her father's fanatics? But no, it was just a figure of speech. She relaxed and told them the superintendent said it was providence.

"Actually, it's fool's luck. I didn't have a hope of finding an opening close to Bentley Falls this late in the summer, but I asked and there it was. English yet, the one department most easily filled."

"Not around here," Alexander Gore said. "Physical Education has that honor. And while they are usually certified to teach another subject, it's too often certified but not able."

"Another of your smashing generalities, brother." Nancy smiled at Kate. "He's given to those—unfair ones—you'll notice that."

"At least I draw my conclusions from working with several phys. ed. majors. Yours come from dating one."

"Ah, but he was able." Nancy's eyes twinkled at them. "Come and have lunch. I've set the table out back."

Out back meant under the branches of a maple tree, at a round table set with a yellow cloth, white dishes with daisies around the edge—it was welcoming. They ate the salad and rolls Nan had prepared, and drank the iced tea, and little by little Kate discovered things about the pair. Nancy, she thought, was about her own age, while Alexander might be anywhere from twenty-seven or -eight to—thirty? That they loved each other was certain. The teasing never had barbed undercurrents, was always good-natured. She learned that Nan had finished college and promptly came down with rheumatic fever and been in bed for months. She would be teaching this year, a first grade in a nearby school, for the first time. Their parents had died, three months apart, when Nan was twenty. An older brother moved to Idaho. "I thought he'd gone out of his head," Alex said, "until we went to visit early this summer. Then we realized he had his head very well together. In fact, we almost stayed."

"But we had this farm."

"Not really a farm," Alex corrected. "But—"

"And lucky we moved here before we saw Idaho. Otherwise—" Nan shook her head. "We have a creek," she said.

"Runs across the back, out through the woods. Fifteen acres. I'm letting it grow back except for the garden."

Kate was taken for a walk through the garden, told to come back when the corn was ready, which would be soon. They walked along the creek, with its trickle of water. "But you should see it in the spring," Nan said. "It's a river, then." By the time Kate drove the Chevy out the drive and back down the road toward the school, she felt sure of one thing. Ford Township School had a sound principal and the sound principal had a nice sister, and she liked both of them. It could be a good year for her, if she stayed.

She was not that sure about her father. Christ Church came into the conversation, as it naturally would, and Nan had asked, cautiously, if Mr. Thorne was aware of the trouble there.

"Nonsense!" Alex emphasized his word with his glass, hitting it hard on the table. "A few people upset because a few other people have discovered religion. I doubt if more than a dozen people know."

"But you do." Kate was curious. "Are you members? Are you part of the few people, the fanatics?"

"Good Lord, no—"

"We are members, sort of—"

"But we don't take sides—"

"Simon says—"

"What we mean to say—" Alex squelched his sister with

a fierce look, dissolving into laughter. "We mean to say that we are members, I taught in Bentley Falls for two years, this will be my third out here. We joined then and we still belong, at least the canvassers find us every fall with their little pledge cards. But we don't take sides. For one thing, we don't really care about other people's religion."

"That sounds awful." Nancy frowned at him.

"Well, it wasn't what I meant to say." He took a bite of roll and chewed it thoughtfully and began again. "I mean we believe in 'Live and let live,' as far as religion is concerned. If I want to say my prayers while I hoe the corn on a Sunday morning, that's my business."

"But you don't. Simon says—"

"You will find, Miss Thorne, that my sister is prone to beginning sentences with the words of that old game. Only in this case she really wants to quote a friend of ours, name of Simon, who—"

"Who would say you really only hoe, you don't pray at all." Nancy sat back, triumphant.

"Simon doesn't know everything. He plays superior tennis, but he doesn't know everything."

"That's the real rub, Kate—may I call you Kate?" Nan paused, and Kate nodded, pleased. "Alex and Simon played every week, as often as they could, and in the winter they bowled, and played chess together, and then Simon found, he met— Well, they were contented bachelors, and then Simon—it's as though he'd met a new girl, only worse."

"Have you ever noticed, Kate Thorne, how people have trouble saying Jesus Christ? Even people like my sister, who attended Sunday school every Sunday until she was old enough to choose, and then very sensibly stopped? She is trying to say that Simon discovered Christ and religion as being suddenly more important than anything else. He received the Baptism in the Holy Spirit—I think that's what they call it—and now he prays in another tongue, God knows what. And he attends prayer meetings not because it is a duty, but because he wants to. He spends Saturday nights driving to far places to hear speakers tell of their experiences—testimony they call it. Last January he was reading a novel, a well-received, pleasantly pornographic best seller. His book mark is still in the place. He hasn't opened it since. His reading now consists of the Bible and testimony from other Christians. His conversation is daily becoming more limited. He also believes that if I broke my leg right now, and he laid hands on me and asked God to heal it at once, God would."

"Try it, I'll call Simon."

"Thanks, no. Don't I recall from somewhere that it is not meet to test the Lord?" Alex laughed. "At any rate, Kate, he is totally involved, and happy about it. He glows with well-being, even without our usual workouts on the courts, and I both envy him and hate him." He tapped his fork on the daisy plate, thinking, then added, "And for all that, he's the best friend I have or could want."

"Simon must be the man who came to our door last night. Does he look as though he were named Mike Murphy?"

Alex nodded, and Kate explained, "He brought a platter of chicken, and I noticed his glow. Even in yesterday's heat, he looked cool."

"That's our Simon, and he's a reasonably good example of the whole charismatic group."

"Why charismatic, I wonder?" Nancy looked puzzled.

"Something about 'charisma' meaning gifts from God, and they claim to receive special gifts from God," Kate said.

"As in tongues." A look of distaste crossed Alex's face. "We don't know who is right or wrong, but Christ Church should be large enough to hold them all."

"I suppose so," Nancy said, "but the thing is, it doesn't sound like Christ Church, you know? When we first went there, I noticed this tremendous dignity about the services and the people. I don't mean that other churches we've attended weren't dignified, but our ministers did tend to arrange the services to suit the mood. At Christ Church they have a pattern, they—oh, you know what I mean," she finished, lifting her hands in despair. "I can't explain, but people aren't emotional, there. They aren't cold, exactly, but—"

"Better stop while you're ahead, little sister. In fairness to Simon, he insists the charismatics aren't emotional, either. He says it's the most real experience he's ever had in his life, and I quote. But the problem is that the charismatic group are eager to share—they're evangelistic and they come on a bit strong. Especially for people like our Mrs. Wyndham. Have you met Grace Wyndham?"

Kate shook her head. The name was familiar, but—

"That's because the church secretary is her niece, Leah Wyndham. A little mouse who keeps quoting Aunt Grace." Nancy giggled. "Poor Leah."

"We should all be so poor." Alex shrugged and stood up. "Come see our garden," he said.

Kate drove along the road, reviewing this conversation in her mind, wishing they'd talked longer about Christ Church. Actually, she supposed she was lucky they'd talked at all; she'd sensed the drawing back in Alex when he learned her father was a minister. Or perhaps she imagined it.

Kate's foot let up on the accelerator; she must make a decision. The question was not Alexander Gore's opinion of ministers' daughters, but whether to go back to the county seat and sign a contract, or go home and think about it for another day.

She drove to the county seat.

Chapter Five

MARGARET THORNE lit the oven, plugged in the mixer, and measured the ingredients for a chocolate cake.

Pete lounged in a chair tipped against the wall, eating a peanut butter sandwich, holding a pop bottle and talking. Squares of colored paper covered the end of the table where Nora sat, folding a green piece, her thin face tight with concentration.

"You sifted flour onto my red paper," she said without looking up. "Gosh, mother—"

Margaret cheerfully suggested that those who use the kitchen table for paper folding take their chances, and Nora might fold paper elsewhere. The door opened, and Kate came in.

"That bottle, Peter dear, looks the perfect answer to the day," she said. "If you love me, you'll get me some of that."

Pete explained it was the last bottle. "So if you don't mind, I just won't love you today," he said.

Margaret poured a glass of lemonade for Kate, then waited until the glass was emptied before she asked about her day.

"I signed a contract," Kate said.

"Oh." Margaret stood still, smiling. "Is it here, in town?"

"Out west, actually. In the middle of nowhere." Kate pointed toward the front door, and told them about the fat superintendent and providence, the sound principal and his pretty sister. "What went on here, while I was gone? Many boxes unloaded, I trust?"

"Mrs. Wyndham came to call," Nora said. "She's a very enigmatic person."

Kate looked startled, and Pete laughed.

"The brat means she is an old lady who drives a black Thunderbird," he explained. "What an old lady wants with that car—"

"She is not an old lady, Pete." Margaret tried to sound properly reproving. "She isn't a lot older than I am, and I am not—"

"She's eons older than you are, and she talks funny."

"That's quite enough. She has an educated accent. She graduated from Radcliffe, Kate. And it wouldn't hurt you to listen and learn, Peter Thorne. Now out, before you spoil your supper."

That, of course, was an impossibility, but he grinned and strolled out the door.

"Mrs. Wyndham is Leah's aunt, Kate. They came back from Spain yesterday. You'll meet Leah soon, I'm sure. She was in the office early this morning. And Mrs. Wyndham is very nice."

Margaret closed her lips firmly and turned the mixer on. Kate considered Nora.

"What, exactly, are you doing?"

"Origami. I learned at camp. Do you know there is not a girl my age in this whole town?"

"She means on this block," Margaret said. "Cheer up, honey, you'll find friends. It takes time."

"Never. There isn't anyone, and I'll probably die of loneliness before summer is over." She looked as though the idea appealed to her, then suddenly raised a smiling face.

"Look, it worked! This is a frog, see?" She held up a piece of green paper, folded into something—it had legs dangling—it was a frog. "And this is a hat," she said, picking up a folded pink paper. "And a crane."

"Oh—the crane! I remember. Japanese paper folding." Kate reached for the orange crane and flipped the wings. "We had a Japanese girl at school one quarter. She showed us how to do the crane and—" Kate paused, searching her memory. "Yes, the crane. She told us that if we made a thousand cranes, our wishes would come true."

"A thousand?" Nora stared, her naturally large eyes widened as she considered this odd idea. "What would you do with a thousand of them? And how could you? It took me ages to make that one."

"You'd string them up, I suppose. But I think there must be easier ways to make one's wishes come true. Better ways."

"And quicker ways," Margaret added, slipping the cake into the oven. "At the rate I'm going, dinner will never be ready. Everybody out, papers too, Nora."

"I'll change my clothes and come help," Kate said and went upstairs.

"A thousand cranes would be an awful lot, wouldn't it?"

Nora gathered her colored papers into a heap. "I don't suppose a person could ever make a thousand."

"I don't suppose a person should try. All that time fooling around, folding paper, when you could be out and doing."

"Yes, but there isn't anyone to be out and doing with." Nora's voice floated back as she went up the stairs. "Not anyone at all."

Poor Nora! Margaret pulled the stool from beneath the table, perched on it and began to snap beans into a pan. Mrs. Wyndham's gardener had picked these today, brought them to the back door shortly before Mrs. Wyndham herself came to the front. But she would not think about Grace Wyndham.

Nora will find friends, if she will be patient. School begins in four weeks; she'll meet all the young people then. And how lucky that Kate chose today to look for a job. Thank You, Lord—I hope Mrs. What's-her-name is happy in Texas, because I'm so glad Kate will be here. Bentley Falls may be the perfect place for Kate. She never would meet young people in Cleveland, all the teachers married, and as for John, he hasn't heard any complaints yet, about those strange awful things. Those people.

Of course, the ones who hated it may all be away now, vacationing. Mrs. Wyndham wasn't angry, this afternoon. She was gracious and charming.

Margaret dropped the ends of a bean into the pan and fished them out, frowning. Not charming. Mrs. Wyndham tried to be, however, and should have credit for that.

She checked the little cake—it was almost done—and put some water with the beans. Mrs. Wyndham might turn out to be her best friend in Bentley Falls, who could tell? Just because she was unpleasantly plump, with fat cheeks and too small eyes, and blew her nose too often—an allergy, she said—and wore a pink and white knit that cost a hundred dollars easily and wasn't a very pretty knit at that—

No, Mrs. Wyndham was not likely to be her best friend, but she wouldn't rule out the possibility. Everything was too new. Even getting dinner in this kitchen took more time than it should, because she wasn't used to it. Hadn't, most likely, put things where they ought to be, for speed.

Upstairs, in the smallest of the four bedrooms, the one with pink walls and woodwork, Nora began her third crane. This went more quickly. She knew where to fold the paper now and—there—pull out the head, and another bird was done, ready to fly. But a thousand of them? She didn't have enough origami paper to make a thousand, and besides, in this dismal town, no one in it but little brats and big kids like Pete, her wishes would never come true.

Not even if she made a million cranes. She stared out the window at the back of the stone church, decided it was even uglier than she'd expected it to be, and then began, slowly, to fold the fourth crane.

Chapter Six

PETE RETURNED the blue casserole to Mrs.
Spencer on Thursday, and came back saying the section on
the hill southeast of town was certainly his kind of place,
the houses brand-new and the cars sitting around, wow!
"But Mrs. Spencer," he said, and laughed, and told them to
get acquainted for themselves.

"She did say she intended to adore every one of us," he
said. "My God, all of us!"

Margaret told him it was not necessary to call on God
for something so foolish, and Kate asked if he was sure Mrs.
Spencer meant to love him, too.

"Me, especially. She plied me with cookies." He
sprawled full length on the sofa, dangled the car keys above
his head. "I'll just keep these, in case you have other errands
for me," he said.

"Only one," Kate said. "To return my keys."

On Sunday, she went to church, wearing one of Margaret's hats, a natural straw with a blue and green scarf tied around it, making a costume of her beige linen dress. John slipped back to the rectory for a quick bite after the eight o'clock communion service, and found her standing before the hall mirror considering the outfit.

"You needn't go," he said, "unless you want to."

"Well, I do. I really want to. Wouldn't you look silly, people asking where your older daughter was, they were sure she was back from school? And you answering that I was at home reading the funnies?"

"People aren't as blunt as that."

"Since when? At least a dozen would ask outright, and another dozen would imply it."

"I wouldn't tell them you were reading the funnies, anyhow. I can dissemble."

"Lovely word, but not proper for the parson. I will be at church."

He looked glad, she thought, and that was her reason for going, so that was settled. Leaning forward, she adjusted the hat and studied the new angle.

"Ah, Narcissus!" Pete came down the steps, grinning.

"Narcissus was a man, naturally." She looked at him in the mirror, blinked and turned to see if it was real. "You'd certainly brighten up a drab morning, but don't you think, with the sun shining and all—"

"I like to look my best for church," he said modestly.

"Of course, but will she be there?"

"Darned right, and she won't be able to miss me in this."

"Absolutely true," Kate agreed. The jacket was a plaid of green and gold, and quite good-looking. But how could Pete be certain a particular girl would be in church?

As they sang the doxology, Kate glanced at Pete, and

learned the answer to her question. He sang with his eyes on the organist, and the organist was a girl. Not just a girl, but a beautiful one, with a streak of light in her long brown hair and eyes that fairly sparkled in the light from the sanctuary.

"She must be years too old for you," Kate whispered, and he shook his head, insisted that wasn't true.

"A junior, just like me," he said. Later, after the benediction, he hastily explained to Kate that her mother was the regular organist, but Judy played once in a while. Kate assured him she admired the way he had not wasted a moment since arriving in Bentley Falls, and he said, "Certainly not," and sneaked out the back way toward the choir room.

For the present moment, however, he settled down to listen to his father's sermon, and to watch the bright streak of hair which was all he could see, sitting down. She was something special, this Judy Lawson, but he wasn't sure why. He didn't, really, care why.

Kate listened, too. She liked the way her father preached, as if he believed every word he said.

As if he did? Kate sighed a little and wiggled into a more comfortable position. He did believe every word, or he wouldn't say them. His text this morning was that bit about how lucky, how blessed, were those who had seen Jesus, and believed, but how much more blessed were those who had not seen, and still believed. She looked around at the people who were listening. Not many hats anymore, she noted. Did they all believe? It would be nice if they did. It would be nice if she did, but after all, look at this world. Suppose there was a God and he'd given his people free will, wouldn't any sensible God have taken it back, long before now?

She turned her head slightly, feeling protected by the

brim of the straw hat, and saw Simon's red head across the church. His face glowed with a light that did not entirely come from the sun, shining through the colored glass. He was a believer, all right, and pleased about it.

Nancy Gore sat beside him, Kate saw, and beyond Nancy sat Alex, his face turned toward the window.

Kate looked back at her father; he was making his last point now, drawing his ideas together. Kate knew, from the silence around her, the feeling in the air, that the congregation listened, and she was glad.

After the service, she stood beside Margaret, meeting people. Three different women exclaimed, "Of course, my dear, you look exactly like your father," and Kate raised her brows in mock distress each time. Did they suppose she was flattered? Alex, Nancy, and Simon waited until the crush was over, until most of the people were downstairs drinking coffee, or out the double doors in the sunshine, before they came up. Kate introduced them to her mother. Margaret and Nancy fell into a sudden discussion of summer fabrics and Kate turned to Simon, standing behind her.

"Your father exhibits the fruits of the spirit in splendid measure," he said, smiling.

"He does?"

"My large friend means that your father preaches a fine sermon." Alex Gore was laughing at Simon, and Kate smiled.

"I agree, he does," she said.

"If he preaches like that often, he'll bring people here closer to Christ than they've ever been before," Simon said.

"Then you and your little gang can capture them." Alex rocked back on his heels, mocking Simon. "Beware, Kate Thorne."

"You're confusing her," Simon said. "Instead, let's

kidnap her for dinner. We're driving up to the lake. We'll have dinner and a swim, then walk up the beach to meet the sunset."

"Poetic fellow," Alex said.

Kate wondered if she should. Was it a good idea to socialize with one's new principal, before school started? Nancy said it wouldn't be that poetic.

"But do come, bring along a pair of shorts and a bathing suit."

"And a tennis racket," Alex said.

"Hiking shoes."

"And a sandwich, in case they cop out on the dinner," Nancy added. "Will you come?"

Kate glanced at Alex; he was smiling. Nancy shook her elbow.

"Of course you will," she said. "Don't look at Alex as though he had any say in the matter. He isn't your boss until next month, remember?"

"Oh, well, in that case!" Kate questioned Margaret with a glance.

"Of course go, Kate. We're having a get-acquainted day with the Sunday school teachers. You needn't come to that."

"Nora?"

"Nora will find something to do."

"Folding cranes?"

"Oh, I hope not!" Margaret followed the last choir members down the steps to join the coffee drinkers. Simon suggested that they avoid the crowd by using the back stairs, and they did, coming out in the lower hall beside Mr. Thorne's office. Kate decided she'd better explore the parish house more thoroughly. She hadn't known the back stairs existed.

There were fifty-nine cranes hanging across Nora's room. Kate stopped to look at them when she went upstairs. She always stopped, because the sight of the brightly colored cranes amused her. They were numbered in black ink.

"You sneaked out too, I see. Are you really planning to make a thousand?"

"Don't be stupid." Nora was struggling to get out of her Sunday dress; her voice came fuzzily through the material. "I hate cranes! I hate dresses, and I hate Bentley Falls!"

"Oh, come on."

"Yes, I do. Are you going somewhere? Can I come along?"

"I am and you can't, but I'll be back. We'll do something together tonight if I get back in time."

"But you won't." Nora sat down on the bed, all thin arms and legs and tangled, long brown hair. "You won't. I saw you talking to those men. You're going with them, aren't you?"

"Yes, but—"

"So you won't get back until the Lord knows when, I don't. I'll have to watch television, and I hate television!"

"Listen, Nora, maybe I'd better not—"

"Shut up. Just shut up and go, I don't care." Nora pushed her hair back, and a gleam of laughter showed in her eyes. "I'll survive, you know. Dad says one rarely dies of boredom. Of course, I could be the exception."

Kate went on to her room, filled her red-striped beach bag with suit and towel, sunglasses and lotion, pulled her racket out of the closet and went downstairs. Nora's voice followed her.

"I also hate people who play tennis without me."

"I challenge you to a game tomorrow," Kate called back.

"Good. But you needn't think you'll win."

Kate didn't think any such thing. She knew better. Nora had taken tennis lessons early last spring, and played every day until they moved—one more reason why she hated Bentley Falls.

"Did you bring a scarf?" Nancy looked up from the magazine section of the paper when Kate came down. "I forgot to mention that Simon is driving his wicked red car, and you'll need a scarf."

"My hair is short—"

"Yes, but he never puts the top up unless it's raining or snowing, and sometimes not even then. You really need a scarf."

"I'll get one." She found a green polka-dot scarf in a raincoat pocket and came back. "Now I'm prepared for anything but mountain climbing. I don't have a rope."

"That's all right, we haven't any mountains. Alex, couldn't we move to the mountains?"

"You can scale the cliff above the river," he told her, opening the door for them. "If you make that, we'll move to the mountains."

"Idiot, that's shale. I'd kill myself."

"An intriguing possibility," Alex said. Simon looked at Kate and smiled.

"I'm an only child myself," he said. "I find such conversations fascinating. They make me glad my parents thought one of me enough."

"Anyone would think one of you enough," Alex said. As he settled himself beside Kate in the back seat of the car, he added that a little less of Simon would be a good idea. "Then you wouldn't push the seat back so far, and ordinary mortals could find a place for their legs."

Simon threw his head back, laughing. "Praise the Lord," he said, "it's a beautiful day."

And it was. They found a table by a window in the restaurant where they could look out over the lake, but at first Kate watched Simon more than the boats. She was curious. He was the first tongue-speaker she'd ever met. She wondered if he would demonstrate, and decided not to ask.

Nancy and Simon were furiously arguing some nonsensical point, and laughing, when Alex looked at Kate, his eyebrows raised.

"You see?" he said, and lifted his shoulders. Kate leaned across the corner of the table.

"You mean, do I see why you miss him when he's off praying? I do. But why isn't he off today? No evangelists handy?"

"Good question. Simon, old friend—" Alex raised his voice, interrupting Nan. "Why have you honored us with your presence this lovely day? No prayer meeting within a hundred miles?"

"I have to work among the heathen, too," he answered, laughing at Nan's protest. "Someday you good people will open your ears and hear, and I want to be around then. Because—"

"Never mind, Simon. We'll let you know if it ever happens. Which isn't likely. Look!" Nan pointed out the window, at the inlet. "Isn't that Larry Spencer's boat?"

"They all look alike to me."

"Yes, but that's Isobel, see?"

Kate leaned forward quickly. This would be the I. Spencer of the unusual telephone call. All she could see was a very thin person, all arms and legs like Nora, with short black hair.

"Of course that's Isobel." Nan went on. "Poor thing, Larry adores his boat, but she gets seasick."

After dinner, they changed into bathing suits and

walked far down the beach. Simon said it was a choice between children throwing sand and the rocky beach, and for his part he would take the rocks. Near the fence that marked the end of the public beach, they spread blankets and settled down.

"Sleep first," Nan said. "It may be an old wives' tale, but the hour isn't up and that dinner deserves to be digested." She lay down, a slim figure in red against the gray blanket. Simon stretched out beside her.

Alex walked to the water's edge, crouched down to study the stones, pick some up and drop them again, and Kate sat watching. The sun spread warm fingers of heat over her body, like a giant hand warming her. For no reason, except perhaps the sun, the warmth, she thought about David. Sometimes it was hard to remember his face, exactly. That frightened her, but she remembered his fine yellow hair, the expression in his eyes when he heard a line of music that was exactly right, and the tone of his voice when he said, "Kate, I love you."

Shivering, she pushed him into her mind's far corner and thought about her companions. Simon must be depressed some days, but today he was joyful. Nancy glowed in his presence, and Kate wondered if she loved him; it seemed most likely. As for Alex, he was pleasant and friendly but Kate knew he kept part of himself aloof, and that was because she was a preacher's kid. Or maybe because he was happy as a bachelor, and more than slightly suspicious of a spinster. Which is what I am, she thought, and giggled.

He wandered back and sat beside her on the army blanket. His skin was deeply tanned to the top of his black trunks. The tan on his legs was much lighter.

"You don't have a farmer's neck," she said, and he asked what a city girl knew about farmers' necks.

"I work without a shirt, most of the time," he said.

"But not in shorts." She was looking at his left leg, where a light scar ran jaggedly down. He looked, too.

"I didn't move fast enough," he said, as though she had asked. "Funny, they teach you to defend yourself from all sorts of danger, but when the guy holding the grenade is ten years old and looks like he's starving, you forget—"

Kate swallowed hard. "In Vietnam, Alex?"

"Eight months and four days. That kid with the grenade is responsible for my staying in school work. I'd had it with education when I went into the army, but this kid haunted me."

Kate thought the kid haunted him still; he leaned back on his elbows, his face turned to the sun, and his lips drawn back tight as though remembering pain. As she watched, they relaxed, and he turned his head toward her.

"Long time ago," he said, and changed the subject. Looking her up and down, laughing, he said it was lucky she wouldn't be wearing that yellow suit to school. "Cause a riot," he said.

Kate glanced down. The one-piece suit glowed against her tan; she was thankful her figure allowed her to wear it. But it was perfectly ordinary, this suit. Had it been a bikini, now—she raised her eyes to meet his and was trapped, unable to move her eyes, to look away. For the first time since David's last leave she was conscious of being desirable, and of desire. She was shocked at the response growing inside herself, the tightened muscles of her stomach, the ache that grew, the yearning.

"He's not entirely a happy bachelor," she thought, forcing herself to think, and heard her own voice say that the sun was hot, wasn't it? Alex answered, said it certainly was.

"The hour must be up, we could go swimming," he said with his mouth, while his eyes—

"They're whispering. Wake up, Simon, they're telling secrets!"

Nancy sat up, shook dark hair from her face. Alex rolled over, closed his eyes, and Kate pulled her knees up, lay her head on them, and smiled across at Nancy.

"We didn't want to waken you," she said, and Nancy said she always woke up when people whispered.

"One of her more unpleasant traits," Alex said, his eyes still closed. "I remember once when I belonged to a very, very secret society, there were thirteen of us in it, all aged thirteen. We thought it was a lucky number. It wasn't; we always fought. Anyhow, this sister of mine discovered—"

He was interrupted by that sister, who reached across Simon and poured sand on his back. He grabbed her arm. "C'mon, let's go swimming!" Yanking her upright, he ran with her across the beach. Kate watched, a smile on her lips and fury inside—what a stupid, ridiculous thing to happen, why didn't I look away immediately? Why didn't he? If he'd leaned one inch closer— I wanted— She buried her face in her arms. Let's face it, Kate Thorne, you're a woman, but brought up in the wrong family.

"All right, Kate?" Simon sat up and Kate opened her eyes, raised her face to answer.

"Fine, of course. Have a good sleep?"

"Not sleep, exactly. Just praising God for sunshine. They make a pair, don't they?" He nodded at Alex and Nancy, splashing each other in the lake.

"Nice pair, though," she said, only half meaning it. If that moment had to happen, why not with Simon? Big, freckled, laughing Simon? His mouth was not drawn back with remembered pain, his red hair—she had nothing against red hair—he was infinitely sexier than Alexander Gore. Why couldn't he look as though he would eat her alive? But he didn't, and he wouldn't.

Kate bubbled up with laughter at herself, and rather than answer the question in Simon's eyes, leaped to her feet and raced toward the water.

Simon followed, loping along, but his legs were long and they reached the water together, dived in together. The water was fiercely cold and sobering. Marvelous.

By the end of the day, Kate was almost able to persuade herself she'd dreamed the moment on the sand. They played at tennis on the beach, without a net but with great spirit and much energy and laughter. They swam, but without the mattress, since no one would sit still long enough to blow it up. They walked to the park for ice cream and pop, and sat on a picnic table eating and talking.

At last they did as Simon first promised, walked westward on the beach to meet the sunset, then turned and strolled slowly back.

On the ride home through the evening world, the radio played soft music, Simon drove slowly, and Kate dozed. She leaned her head back on the seat and fell asleep far away from Alexander Gore. When she wakened, her head was resting on his shoulder, but he was so matter of fact about it, helping her out of the small back seat, carrying her gear to the door, she could say thank you, call back to the others and wave goodbye as though that moment had never occurred.

Perhaps I imagined it, she thought, watching the red car disappear onto Main Street. He may not realize it happened, but—even as she thought those words, she remembered his eyes. He hadn't meant it to happen, and he didn't mean it to happen again, but he knew.

Chapter Seven

KATE MET Isobel Spencer the following Wednesday when she came home from a shopping trip with Nora, her arms loaded with packages. She held the screen back with one foot as Nora went in, and before taking another step was surrounded by flying hands, a high voice saying, "Here, give me the packages. Poor child in all this heat, do let me help." Nora escaped into the kitchen.

"I can manage," Kate said, desperately clutching the bags and trying to keep her balance, but Isobel wrestled them from her grasp and by only spilling one managed to set both bags on the table.

"There," she said triumphantly, and beamed at Kate. Her thin arms resembled rope through the transparent, flowered dress; wispy black bangs floated across her forehead. Her expression was that of a proud puppy who chewed only half the slipper before presenting it to his master. Kate almost reached out to pat her head, say "There, there."

"I'm Isobel Spencer, and you must come in and sit. Such a hot day to walk downtown, even though it isn't far. You must be exhausted, really. Your mother is getting tea. I told her she needn't, for me, but she insisted. She's the dearest soul—do you know how lucky you are?" Dark eyes rolled toward the heavens. "Of course you do, and you are just as pretty as she is. What a fortunate day for Bentley Falls when the Thornes came to stay."

Kate couldn't think of an answer to any of that, so permitted herself to be led to a chair and a pillow put behind her head. She settled for smiling.

"And that was darling Nora with you, wasn't it? She'll be just like your mother when she grows up. They look alike already, lucky Nora." Mrs. Spencer jumped up to help Margaret with the tea tray; Kate was sure that would be a disaster and closed her eyes, but Margaret was quicker than she had been, and more prepared of course. The tray landed safely on the coffee table, nothing spilled. Mrs. Spencer talked on.

She talked and drank tea and ate cookies. Kate decided their guest had recently stopped smoking; she reached for a cookie more often than she needed them, sometimes holding one in each hand.

"And you are going to teach here in Rivers County." Isobel Spencer actually clapped her hands. "Your mother told me about it. I'm so glad. That's the leading of the Lord, you know. He has great plans for you, I feel that."

Kate's mouth opened and closed again, her words unsaid. (The Lord didn't have a damn thing to do with it, and you may go to blazes, she thought, and crunched her cookie.)

Mrs. Spencer finished her second cup of tea. "You know

why I've come," she said. "Or no, you don't. I've come to talk about— Well, I wondered, your dear husband, your father. Mr. Thorne. I will call him Mister, you see, although we always said Reverend." She smiled at Kate. "We wondered how he felt— We hoped— Oh, dear."

She reached a full stop. Kate looked at Margaret. Margaret nodded her head and said, "Yes, of course," and poured Mrs. Spencer a third cup of tea.

"You see, it's our prayer group. There are some people —or do you know about our group already? The members come from all different churches, but really lovely people. They all love the Lord, you see. It means so much to me, but Larry—" she groped for words, then set her cup down with a bang. "Larry thinks it is a disgrace. He says I shouldn't go. But if Mr. Thorne approves, if he speaks up for it— Do you think he will?"

Margaret reached out and patted her hand. Kate wished herself upstairs, but not being a magician, she was stuck in the green chair and speechless.

"You want to talk to John about it," Margaret said, and Mrs. Spencer nodded.

"Yes, to Mr. Thorne. I really must; it means the world to me. I thought though, if I talked to you first, you being a woman. Does Mr. Thorne listen?" She asked the question wistfully, and Kate felt guilty. Larry Spencer was not a listener, she inferred.

"Larry comes to church, you know. Every Sunday. But not because he loves the Lord." She paused; Kate and Margaret were listening. "Because he loves the church. Not the Body of Christ which is the real church, we know that, but the stones. The stones Christ Church is made of, and the windows— He walks about each week checking to be sure nothing has happened to his church. If it burned down one day, he'd be lost."

"He'd help build a new one," Margaret said, hoping to ease the burden she carried, but this brought tears to the dark eyes in the thin face.

"Yes, perhaps he would. And then he would love those stones even more. He thinks because he loves Christ Church, because he comes to church nearly every Sunday and listens—although I don't think he really does listen, you know—he thinks he is a Christian. And he isn't." She leaned forward. "He has never accepted Christ as his Savior, you see."

Margaret looked startled. "He wasn't confirmed?"

"Of course, when he was thirteen. What does a thirteen-year-old know? He's never met the Lord."

Kate resisted the temptation to ask Mrs. Spencer when she'd had the pleasure; it would have been too rude. But this was all a bit much. She said she would check, see if her father was back, and walked out. Her mother's eyes sparkled, calling her coward silently, but after all, mother married the preacher. She could cope.

Nora sat at the kitchen table refreshing herself with a stack of cookies and a glass of something with ice in it. Kate went on through, out the door and across the rectory yard. As a car door slammed, she turned back and intercepted her father as he headed for his office.

"No peace for even the least wicked, love. Mrs. Spencer wants to talk to you in the house."

"Not yet. I've just come from the hospital, Kate. I need time—"

"It fits. Mrs. Spencer is sick, too. Mother is coping, but she needs you."

He sighed and went back to the house. Kate challenged Nora to a game on the city courts, three blocks away. As they came quietly down the stairs, rackets in hand, and went down the back hall toward the kitchen, she heard Isobel talking, talking—

"Since I've received, Reverend Thorne, since I accepted the gifts of the Spirit the Lord freely gives, my whole life has changed, my whole world has changed. But Larry thinks I'm insane. He thinks I should see a psychiatrist."

And who could blame him? Kate grinned, but without humor in her heart. Thank God, John Thorne believes. He loves the same Lord Mrs. Spencer loves, though I've never heard him claim an actual speaking, gift-exchanging relationship. But he believes, and he will take care of her. He'll help, thank God—

Kate stopped on the lowest step, listened to her own thoughts and laughed at herself. Nora waited.

"What's so funny?"

"Me. Thanking someone I don't know exists, for sure."

Later that evening, Kate asked her father about Isobel. He was working out a chess problem; frowning, he moved the white knight before he answered.

"If I'd had a choice, I would have chosen the kind of mind that solves problems like that." He snapped his fingers, and moved the white knight back again. "Chess puzzles and people puzzles, too. Isobel Spencer. She's a member of the charismatic group. She prays in tongues, and her husband thinks she is mad. That's the whole problem, and that's quite a problem. I've met Larry Spencer."

"She says he adores Christ Church."

"He does. Adores is exactly the word. He knows exactly where every crack in the plaster is. He probably knows when each light bulb was put in and how many light hours each has left. Isobel couldn't care less about the building. She has given herself entirely to following Christ. She's found a new master, and no amount of arguing could convince her otherwise."

"Have you tried?"

"Good heavens, no." John leaned back in his chair; he held a white bishop in his hands, rubbing it between his fingers. "In the first place, this personal Pentecost may be real. God knows, I don't. It seems real to them. You can't argue with personal revelation, Kate, don't you know that? If Isobel says she has met the Lord, and He has given her a new tongue with which to praise Him, I can only be thankful."

"Thankful?" Margaret looked up from the scarlet sweater she was knitting for Nora. "How can you be thankful, John?"

"Maggie, I praise God for anything that brings people closer to Him. And this does. Of course, it would be nice if every member of Christ Church could have the same experience, on the same day. Then it would create love instead of hate."

"Why hate?" Kate interrupted him, frowning. Hate seemed a strange word to connect with Simon or Isobel.

"I suppose I really meant fear. But fear comes out as hate, looks like hate, in action. When people feel threatened, you know—" He put the bishop on the board and moved the entire chess table to the side of his chair, with a sigh. "Tomorrow morning, Kate, how would you like to play secretary? I have some typing I want done, and Leah is busy with an extra mailing."

Kate accepted. She enjoyed typing for her father, and over the years had learned to decipher his handwriting with ease. Well, usually with ease. When he was really into his subject, he got carried away and scribbled so fast that no one short of God Himself—Kate laughed. If she really intended to live at home this year, and she did, she would have to stop using God's name so casually.

The next morning she walked across the backyard with John Thorne, through the gap in the hedge and the back door of his office. He gave her a sheaf of papers, thick with pencil writing, crossed out, sentences added, wedged in—

"Ever consider going back to third grade, daddy? They teach cursive writing about then."

"Don't be disrespectful, child. Sit down and type."

She settled herself at the table near the back window. John opened the door leading into the hall, and went into the next office. Kate heard Leah's high voice, giggling, telling him about the weather as though he hadn't been out in it.

"So terribly hot, Mr. Thorne. It'll have to break soon, don't you think? Aunt Grace says it will."

Kate stopped listening. Nancy Gore did not exaggerate Leah's fixation on Aunt Grace. Kate suspected every mirror at Leah's house was filled with pictures of Aunt Grace. Certainly Leah looked as though she never saw herself: no makeup at all, hair pulled back into an elastic band, heavy, dark-rimmed glasses and high-necked dresses—Leah Wyndham, the niece of Aunt Grace.

"I'll bring the mail in as soon as it comes, Mr. Thorne."

John came back to the office and made a phone call. As he hung up the receiver, Leah tiptoed into the room.

"Several calls came in yesterday after you'd gone, and I took these messages, and then three letters came. You ought to answer them—" she held them out almost reluctantly. Kate, who had been watching from the corner of her eye, turned completely around.

"Wouldn't it be better if I took this work on home?"

"Stay here, Kate. It's cooler."

"Oh, yes, Miss Thorne, the heat outside is awful."

"Kate—won't you call me Kate?"

"Yes, thank you, of course I will." She fluttered her fingers and turned back to the minister. "Christine Blanshard called."

"Yes, she called Mrs. Thorne. Have I met them yet?"

"They weren't in church Sunday. I remember missing them. Probably visiting their children. Of course, it isn't for me to say, Mr. Thorne, but Aunt Grace says they're fanatics." She whispered the last word. "They were perfectly ordinary people when they first came here. I mean, she taught Sunday school—I had her myself in the eighth grade. Their boys were confirmed in the church. But after the last one went to college, something happened."

Kate sat with her fingers on the keys, waiting. She ought to type but it seemed rude, and besides—

"It used to be they wanted social affairs, fellowship, you know, all the time. And now—" Leah's voice dropped again. "Now they have prayer meetings."

She might have said pot parties, or drunken orgies in that tone. It was impossible not to smile.

"It isn't funny, Mr. Thorne. Aunt Grace says—"

"Does Mrs. Wyndham attend the meetings?"

"Oh, goodness, no! They talk crazy, and they pray for people to get well when they're sick—"

"But Leah, shouldn't we all do that?"

"Yes, but I heard they put oil on someone's forehead and put their hands on them, and they expect the people to get well!"

"Do they?" He sounded wistful, Kate thought.

"Well, I don't know. It's not for me to say. But they pray in languages they can't even understand, Aunt Grace says."

"It's called speaking in tongues, Leah. The early Christians spoke in tongues, you know. You've read the Book of Acts, I'm sure."

"But my goodness, Mr. Thorne, we've come a long way since then, haven't we? I mean, civilization and all?"

"Certainly," he said. "A long way. Now let's see about these letters."

Kate began to type again, hurrying to make up for lost time. Leah went out a little later.

"Just ask Aunt Grace about the Blanshards," she said, turning at the door. "Just ask Aunt Grace."

About eleven someone tapped on the outside door.

"Reverend Thorne?"

"Come in, Martin."

The door opened to admit the sexton. Kate lifted a hand in greeting. Martin was the first member of Christ Church she met, the day after she came home. She liked him. Tall, thin, always wearing a blue sweater with the third button missing, fluffs of white hair floated across the top of his head like tiny clouds, and a pipe always hung from the corner of his mouth—except in the sanctuary. Kate saw him sweeping near the altar one day, and the pipe was gone.

"Them kids have been stopping in again after school, messing up."

Kate grinned. That was another thing about Martin. He grumbled. About everything. But let anyone else say a thing about Christ Church kids, and he'd tear their eyes out.

He grumbled on and Kate typed, until she heard a familiar name.

"Now you know Grace, Reverend. She won't hold still for using the red book when her name's on the black one. And Helen says we ought to use the red every other week on account of her mother—" He paused as Mr. Thorne's laughter rang out, and then he laughed, too.

"Well, yeah," he said. "Women."

"Best thing is not to worry. The ladies will settle it themselves, eventually."

"I hope so. I do hope so." Martin went out, closing the door behind him.

"Poor Martin," John said.

"Poor daddy!"

"Let's go home and eat lunch."

Kate stood up gratefully, and stopped. A flurry of sound, Leah's agitated face and breathless voice announcing Aunt Grace, and Mrs. Wyndham appeared.

The fabled Aunt Grace. Kate acknowledged the introduction and moved toward the door.

"Sit down, Miss Thorne. I see you have work to do, and I shall not keep you from it. I am not on a secret mission. What I have to say I will say to the whole church, if necessary. I trust—" she glared at John Thorne. "I trust it will not become necessary."

"Nice of you to come out on such a hot day, Mrs. Wyndham. I hope you have good news. Your family is fine?"

"If by my family, you mean my daughters, I suppose they are. They do not overwhelm me with letters, but this is typical of their generation. If you mean my son, that is another matter, but I will see to him." Her plump face grew red, her lips made a straight, firm line across it. "You have been here two weeks, Mr. Thorne, and I'm sure you know what is going on. I want it stopped. Christ Church will not become the laughingstock of Bentley Falls."

"I can't imagine people laughing at Christ Church." John eased her into a chair and walked around his desk. His quick glance at Kate told her to sit, too, and wait.

"Christ Church is not the largest church in Bentley Falls," she said. "Nor is it the oldest. Helen Bentley's greatest sorrow is that her ancestor was not a more religious man."

"Miss Bentley is fortunate," John murmured. Grace looked startled.

"Exactly what do you mean?"

"If that's her greatest sorrow," he said, lifting a hand toward the world in general, smiling his small smile. "Today, you know—"

"Yes. Well, perhaps I exaggerated. My point is simply this. Christ Church may not be the largest or the oldest, but we are known for our dignity. For the beauty of our services, the class of our parishioners. Now—I don't mean that we have ever kept anyone out, that we are prejudiced, but we simply do not appeal to certain kinds of people. We reach the better educated, for example, why I, myself am a—" She paused and seemed to decide that all this was irrelevant. "Now we are being invaded—invaded, Mr. Thorne, by a group determined to turn religion into a sideshow. They have no place in Christ Church, yet two of our Board members belong to that group. Two of them!"

"I've heard, but—"

"We hired you, with the Bishop's blessing, because he believed you could stop it, and I want it stopped. I had a call this very morning." She stopped to sneeze, struggled to find a handkerchief, and blew her nose hard. "My allergies," she said. "I've had hay fever since I was ten, and this time of year— But about this call—" she sniffed. "Helen Bentley said that Craig Blanshard, who is *not* a doctor, healed a cross-eyed child."

She blew her nose once more and sat back, glared at her pastor. He looked back. Kate, behind them, waited. How in the hell, she wondered, does an ordinary man heal crossed eyes?

"It's bad enough when they hold their meetings at Camilla Frey's and I hear them singing in my living room. A block away. And the cars along the street, disgusting. And the neighbors ask me, 'Doesn't she go to your church?' Darling Camilla, she's getting old and a little—you know. I tell them that. But I see the Blanshards going to those meetings. Craig is a member of our own Board, you know. I see Dr. Hook going. A medical doctor who ought to know better. Last week I counted ten Christ Church people going to Camilla's house, and I may have missed some. We have rather a large hedge, you know, and even from an upstairs window— There were crowds of people there, and some of them I know from St. Marys. Romans!" She sniffed again, and Mr. Thorne took the opportunity to suggest, gently, that an ecumenical prayer meeting was quite a marvelous thing, that God might well be pleased.

"The ecumenical movement is another thing," she said. "It seems to me that if we were intended to belong to one church—" she caught herself, apparently remembered that that was not the subject of her visit. "Mr. Thorne, Helen Bentley does not lie, and she informed me that Craig healed this child. She sat in a chair and they spilled oil on her—"

"Now, Mrs. Wyndham—"

"The eyes were crossed and now they are straight. Helen said it happened. And you know that cannot happen." She stopped to sniff once more. "Now, you may stand for this nonsense, but I will not. I shall expect you to—"

Mr. Thorne interrupted with an unusually firm tone.

"Mrs. Wyndham, you and I know that Craig Blanshard cannot heal anyone's eyes. You and I know that."

She looked at him uncertainly, then nodded.

"I'm going to meet with Mr. Blanshard very soon. I have

an appointment. You let me worry about it, won't you?"
With gentle, reassuring words, he led her out of the room
and down the hall.

Returning, he closed the office door and leaned against
it.

"You have now met our Aunt Grace," he said.

"Yes, but have you really an appointment with Blanshard?"

"Not only an appointment, but a dinner date. We're
going there Saturday night."

Kate chuckled. "Check your eyes first. You may find
yourself being prayed over. Don't you wish you were back at
St. Paul's, where the color of the choir robes caused the
biggest fight?"

"I miss our old friends, but you must admit, Kate, this is
different. A challenge!" He opened the outer door and
followed her into the sunshine. "I'm looking forward to
Saturday night."

"Better you than me," Kate said, and her father
laughed.

"The invitation included you, Kate. She was very
definite about it. 'Be sure and bring Kathryn,' she said."

Chapter Eight

THE WEATHER did break by Saturday night. Kate sat in the back seat feeling damp and wishing she was at home. But it was too late for that. Already they were turning from Main Street onto the North River Road, where the Blanshards lived. She peered through the rain at the old-fashioned portico that sheltered part of the drive. A tall man—Craig Blanshard, no doubt—stood in the doorway, told them to leave the car under the roof and come in, come in. They followed instructions gladly.

Kate caught a glimpse of a little red car with the top up further along the drive, where it circled around the house, and was not surprised to see Simon standing in the hall. She waved and turned to meet her host.

Ordinary. He was just that. Gray hair, a long, lean body covered with a light blue shirt and tie, gray pants, and a lightweight jacket; sharp small crowsfeet crinkled near his eyes as though he smiled with his whole face, often. This was the man who healed crossed eyes?

Christina Blanshard looked ordinary, too. She came from the kitchen with a pink apron covering her white dress, her short dark hair had not begun to gray—or was skillfully rinsed?—and her rather prominent teeth gleamed white as she smiled.

Simon led the way into a living room which obviously doubled as a library; Craig poured wine, very light, he said, and excellent for rainy, summer days, and they sat together and discussed the weather.

Which was, Kate thought, ridiculous. When they went into the dining room a little later, she supposed that now it would come: John the Baptist for an appetizer, Jesus Christ for the main course, and Saint Paul for dessert. Instead, she was offered the Cleveland Indians, the summer theater in all its infinite variety, and for dessert a choice between the men discussing the utilities strike about to be, and the women analyzing the fashion picture for the fall season, with other ordinary subjects tossed in and considered lightly.

Christina brought coffee to the living room, and they sat without conversation then, listening to the rain smashing against the windows, and watching as lightning streaked the room time after time. A comfortable, no-tension silence. Even Simon, whose laughter had punctuated the last hour, seemed content to drink his coffee and wait.

Finally, after a large burst of thunder, Craig put his cup down and turned to John Thorne.

"You have questions, I think," he said.

"Questions?" John seemed to consider the word, turn it around in his mind, before he shook his head slightly. "I have curiosity. Wonder. I don't know enough to ask questions."

Kate, sitting beside Margaret on the sofa, felt her mother stiffen, push herself back. Christina noticed, too, and reached out, touched Margaret's knee.

"It's all right, you know," she said, and Margaret smiled and relaxed again. A flash of lightning held the fireplace suspended in white brightness for a long moment. "Come along, Simon, let's draw these curtains." Chris stood and Simon followed. When they sat down again, Mr. Thorne had finished his coffee.

"If you will," he said, "suppose you tell us about it."

"Yes, but—"

"From the beginning," Mr. Thorne said, firmly.

"We were born," Craig began, and shouted with laughter as he looked at Kate. "No, really, Kate, don't panic. I won't start there. But we were, you know. And were proper church members for years, just as we'd been taught to be when we were small. We broke away during college, of course—doesn't everyone?"

"Not everyone these days," Simon said, and Craig nodded and said that was true, praise the Lord.

"Well, we had three sons and we taught Sunday school and did all the usual things which we ought to do and luckily not too many things which we ought not to do."

"Nice, normal Christian folk," Simon said, his eyes twinkling.

"Exactly. But we were increasingly uncomfortable," Chris added.

"Yes. We talked together, or with friends—not just Christ Church friends but from other places, First Church, the Methodists, even our Catholic friends, and no one seemed to know what was wrong, but we all agreed something was. And then—"

"We had an accident." Chris clapped her hands, as though an accident could be a joyous occasion.

"Yes." Craig looked at his wife, smiling, then turned to consider the Thornes, as though wondering if he should go on. "Well—it was rather dramatic, but it was the beginning. And it is true." He looked around as though expecting a challenge, and Simon said, "Praise God."

"A fellow backed out of his driveway into the path of our car. We weren't hurt, none of the adults were, but his little girl was tossed around in the back seat and her arm was broken."

"It was really broken." Christina leaned forward, now. "I'm a physical therapist, you know. I looked carefully at it, the bones were angled, not through the skin but obviously broken. The child was pale, and she lay in her mother's lap while we waited for the police and—"

"The little girl said that Jesus wouldn't like it, her arm being broken." Craig's lips formed a gentle, remembering smile. "Her mother said indeed, Jesus wouldn't, and she put her hands on that child's arm and prayed. She just asked God to heal that arm, and she claimed the healing in the name of Jesus. She said thank you and then very quietly, so that we could scarcely distinguish the sounds, she prayed in tongues. I mean—"

"I know what you mean," John said.

"Good. At the time, we didn't understand at all. It seemed ridiculous and illogical, you see, and we thought—oh, we thought she was mad. But as we watched, the color came back into the child's cheeks and in a few moments—"

"Just a few moments," Chris said.

"That arm was all right. I mean absolutely one hundred percent all right."

Craig poured himself a cup of coffee. Kate stared at the handle of the pewter sugar bowl. The arm hadn't been broken in the first place, that was obvious. They were upset and imagined it; when the mother prayed in that strange way they— Well, it was simple.

"The police came, and we got the cars sorted out and did all the things one has to do, but Chris and I were more interested in the mother by then. We didn't care much about a crumpled fender; anyone can crumple a fender." He held his cup in both hands, looking at the coffee, smiling. "The mother gave us a book about the rise of the charismatic movement in the mainline churches, the traditional denominations. About thousands of people having their lives changed because they believe in Jesus Christ as their Savior."

"But Craig, surely you believed that already?" John shifted in his chair; he was not smiling.

"Yes—and no. We'd always said we believed it, but let's face it, it didn't mean much to either of us then. But we read the book—it was John Sherrill's *They Speak with Other Tongues*—and when we came to the last page, wondering if this could possibly be the answer for us, the phone rang. It was one of our friends, name of Jim, from First Church, really excited because someone had given him a copy of the same book. He'd just finished reading it and wanted to share it with us."

Kate smiled. "Rather a neat coincidence," she said.

"Not a coincidence. One thing we've learned since letting the Lord come into our lives, is that He works that way. What seems mere chance is not chance at all, but the Lord deliberately putting His hand in, working through us."

What rubbish, Kate thought, but kept her mouth shut. A guest is a guest is a guest.

"What happened then?" Margaret asked. Chris laughed and said, "Everything."

"She's right—everything." Craig laughed too, joyously.

"Our friends came over in a rush—Jim and his wife, Lois—and we talked about it far into the night. We decided that if the experience Sherrill was writing about was real, we wanted it. Finally Jim said he was going to ask, because he'd believed Jesus was his Savior for a long time now. We knelt together, right over there by the fireplace, and he said a prayer. He simply asked Jesus for the gift of His Holy Spirit. He asked to be filled, and he said thank you, and then he praised God." Craig looked at Kate, at Margaret and John. "He was praising God, and all of a sudden he stammered a bit, and began speaking in a language none of us had ever heard before. He knelt there praying, and we sat back on our heels staring at him."

Chris took up the story. "The next day Jim called Craig and asked if it really happened. He couldn't believe it, and Craig said to try it again, in the cold light of day. He did. Right over the phone Jim began to pray in his new and beautiful language." She looked at Kate and grinned. "You don't have to believe us, but it is true, Kate. But don't worry—"

"It sounds silly!" Kate blurted the words, wished them back, decided to go on. "Sounds like over-emotional nonsense, a religion trip. A praying jag."

"True," Simon said. "But it isn't any of those things."

"No." John Thorne shook his head slightly and smiled. "It isn't necessarily any of those things, though it could be any of them. What happened to the rest of you?"

"We couldn't wait to have the experience, too, but obligations kept interfering, and Jim's firm sent him off on an extended trip, that same week. It was the Lord's way, we realize now, of telling us to 'read, learn and inwardly digest' before asking. We met together for several weeks and studied everything we could find. People everywhere are

~ 72 ~

having this experience and writing about it. And the Lord sent people to us."

Kate's cup clattered in her saucer.

"They had a certain special glow, and we wanted what they had. Finally one night we prayed together, eleven of us, and the Lord is good. We asked, and each one of us received a new tongue. We were baptized into the Spirit of the Lord."

There are ways to live through the most impossible situations. As a preacher's daughter, Kate had learned long ago how to appear to be listening while lost in thoughts of her own. She fixed a half-smile on her lips, held her cup in both hands, and thought furiously about Nora and her cranes, two hundred and three, last count. Pete had borrowed her car that night for his date with the organist's daughter, Judy Lawson. She hoped they were having fun. Nora was visiting a friend, a real, live, brand-new friend, after two weeks of despair.

Alexander Gore. That was something to think about. He might have called. But perhaps it was as well that he hadn't. She didn't want to date her principal, not yet. Maybe not ever; certainly not yet.

Beth's husband had come home last Sunday. She hadn't heard, of course, but she hoped they were wonderfully happy.

She was deep in a consideration of what classes she might have next year, what kind of pupils, when someone removed the coffee cup and touched her shoulder.

"How about riding home with me? You haven't heard a word for the past twenty minutes, might as well take the body out."

"But it's all—very interesting."

"I've noticed. Let's go."

She said good night to the Blanshards, who apparently thought it quite normal for someone to leave in the middle of their story. Her father was obviously waiting for her to leave so that he could ask more questions. Even her mother seemed willing to stay.

"I only hope they don't stay too long," Kate said, as Simon slammed the door of the car, shutting the rain outside.

"Afraid it's contagious? Don't worry, your father seems like a very deliberate sort of man. He's seen emotional jags before, and he'll want to be darn sure this isn't that—right? He'll weigh and consider, and eventually—"

"Recognize it for the rubbish it is." She leaned back, waiting for his rebuttal, but he laughed and suggested they go somewhere for something.

"Another cup of coffee and I'd drown," she said. "I'd rather go home, Simon."

"Sure?" She nodded and he drove around the old brick house and turned the car toward town. When they reached the rectory, she invited him in, on one condition: that they talk about ordinary things. Non-controversial topics.

"Politics even, or woman's lib. Promise?"

"Absolutely." Inside he spotted the jigsaw puzzle Nora had started that afternoon, and sat down on the far side of the table, claimed he was an expert. To prove it, he immediately put a piece in place.

"Why not sit in front?"

"My mother always sat in front. I'm conditioned to seeing puzzles upside down, can't do them the right way. But I'm an expert, all the same." He placed another piece and grinned at Kate. "You see?"

"I see." She sat in front of the puzzle and they worked in silence for a time, until Simon leaned back, said even experts must stop sometime.

"Have you seen Alex this week?" He asked lightly, but Kate heard the serious tone beneath and looked intently at him.

"No. Why?"

"Oh, I blew it. The other night, after we dropped you off, I got to talking, got carried away."

"You mean, about—"

"About the charismaniacs, as Alex calls us."

"Charismaniacs? That's lovely!" Kate laughed and sobered quickly; he looked worried.

"Alex and I, we've had thousands of arguments the last ten years, but never anything that kept us from sharing another beer. Somehow Sunday night was different."

"Have you known each other ten years, really?"

"More than that. We met freshman year at school. He looked in Bentley Falls for a job when he finished graduate school, because I was settled here. Had to, you know, because of dad."

"Had to?"

"Well, it seemed as though I had to. An only child has responsibilities, whether he wants them or not. Especially when the father has a flourishing store. You've been in our store?" His eyes wandered over the table as he talked and now he leaned forward, placed a small piece in the puzzle with a triumphant "Ha!"

Kate clapped her hands admiringly. She'd been in Garcia's store, in the center block downtown, the kind of jewelry store where one was tempted to tiptoe and wear white gloves.

"The day I went in, I didn't know it was yours," she said. "I went in because the windows enticed me."

"Thank you, ma'am, I take full credit for that. My father believes that if people know you have the finest selection in town, or in several towns around, they'll come even if you board up the windows. Now me, with my fine education, I believe in using those windows— There." He put another piece in the puzzle. "As for Alex and Nan, their folks moved a dozen times while they grew up; they didn't have a hometown to go back to, so they borrowed mine. Praise the Lord! Except for last Sunday night, but that was my idiocy, not the Lord's."

"Simon, we were all tired that night. I slept all the way home, remember? Alex won't let one argument spoil an old friendship."

"No, I shouldn't think so. But he usually drops in, or Nan calls—" He grinned. "Or I do. But I'm pigheaded, too, I guess."

"He's getting ready for school, you know. He's busy." She tried a piece, discovered it didn't fit and put it back on the table with a disgusted look. Then she laughed. "But charismaniacs? That's beautiful. Especially after tonight, miracles yet. You and the Blanshards!"

"Kate, don't you believe in miracles?"

"My experience with miracles," she said, "has been very slight." So slight she could count them on one finger, and that because she considered being alive at all a kind of miracle. "Broken arms that don't stay broken, and Mrs. Wyndham's story about eyes being healed—that's even worse than the arm."

Simon studied a piece of the puzzle while he whistled something Kate didn't recognize, and then he said she'd heard about that, had she?

"Mrs. Wyndham came in and told dad. It's the most impossible thing I ever heard of."

"Your father would say it wasn't."

"My father said—I heard him—that no man can heal eyes. He said it. No man can heal another person's eyes."

"Certainly not, who's arguing?" Simon's loud laughter

filled the living room. "Kate, no man, except our good doctors, tries to do that. But if God exists at all, He has to be infinite, Kate. He must be able to do anything, so why not heal an arm, or an eye? All it takes is faith. That mother believed God would heal her girl's broken arm, so God did. However—" he snapped his fingers, leaned over the puzzle again. "Let's not argue. I promised I wouldn't mention the subject, remember? And especially let's not discuss Grace Wyndham, poor soul. I hear Walter's come home."

"Who in the dickens is Walter?"

"Her youngest son. Sophomore at State this fall, and according to Craig, he's discovered the Lord *and* the Baptism. Poor Grace!"

Kate remembered Mrs. Wyndham's assurance that she would take care of her son. It might not prove too simple.

"For years, people have listened to Grace brag about Walter," Simon said, fitting another piece into the puzzle. "Now she has something to brag about, but she won't, you can bet on that. Long hair, he wears a cross, and he prays in tongues!"

"I know the type," Kate said, thinking of the last day on campus and the eager pain-in-the-neck she'd encountered. "My sympathies are with Mrs. Wyndham."

"Yes, but Walter's all right. Craig says he has his head together. He'll make her proud yet if she lets him grow up, find his way. The Lord will help him do that."

"Simon, you are cursed with a one-track mind. You'd better go on home, I think. It's getting late."

"Kate, come to prayer meeting."

"Do what?"

"No, seriously. You judge, but you don't know. Come and see for yourself."

Kate stared at him. A date with Simon, yes, she'd like that. But a prayer meeting? God forbid!

"You're afraid."

"Rot. I just don't want to. I'm not interested."

"You ought to know what you aren't interested in."

"After tonight? Thanks, I know."

"Listen, let's make a bet. You come with me to prayer meeting next Friday night. If you still call it nonsense, after that, I'll buy you dinner on Saturday night. On the other hand, if you change your mind, you may treat."

"Simon, that would be the safest bet I'd ever make. But—" there was one thing. "What about Nancy? I mean, you aren't—or anything?"

"Nan?" He looked surprised. "No, not anything. Nan is a doll but— Besides, girl, I only suggested dinner!"

Kate giggled. "I know, but I like her so much."

"So do I."

Kate remembered the way Nancy looked at Simon. She adored Simon, that was no secret. But perhaps adoration wasn't love, and perhaps he was right, she would not be hurt. And it was only dinner, and Bentley Falls offered few entertainments. But a prayer meeting?

"All right, Simon, it's a bet. But I agree with Alex, you're a bunch of charismaniacs. Start saving for that dinner."

"Totally unnecessary. It will be on you. And I'm partial to lobster."

At the door, Kate couldn't resist one last question.

"Does the Lord approve of betting?"

"Well, in a good cause—" Rubbing his fingers through thick, red hair, he grinned at Kate. "I'll ask Him tonight," he said.

Chapter Nine

"KATE THORNE, you were out of your head!" The thought opened her eyes on Sunday morning, and wakened her completely. You don't want to go to a prayer meeting. What in hell have you let yourself in for?

Miracles!

Define the term, Kate—if a miracle is something you don't understand, then yes, there are miracles. Electricity is one. Wood, that grows in a forest and becomes paper and furniture, that's another. A man-made miracle down to a certain point, of course, but at the bottom is the tree itself, which grew from a seed, and man can't make a seed.

God didn't blow his breath into *a* man on *a* particular morning, but still there is something in a man. His soul? His spirit? "My genes made me what I am," she thought, "gift of my parents and their parents. When I pinch myself, I hurt, but if I could toss out that part, the hurting part, would I still be me?"

Damn it all to hell, she thought, and threw the covers back and sat up. The beige dress would do for church again, I guess, it's hot already and only eight-thirty. I wish the cooler weather would come, I really do.

I don't have to believe anything, unless I want to. Miracles or no miracles. I must have been mad to agree to go with Simon. Aren't there any normal people in this town? Maybe there is a God, all right say there is, if He can make trees grow and electricity happen for men to use, He could probably—now, be honest—He could certainly heal a broken arm. If it was broken. He could heal it, and the Blanshards could be given to taking LSD and having hallucinations.

Deciding against the beige dress—she couldn't have people think she owned only one dress—she put on a blue print. After church she slipped down the convenient back stairs and went home, changed into shorts and a blouse and prepared lunch. A breeze blew down from the lake and tempered the sunshine; when Mr. Thorne cut a slice of fresh tomato a little later, he said he was sure that August was the finest month of all, what with the weather, the tomato season, and the peaches just ready.

Pete created a towering sandwich with his meat and tomato. Having asked for and received permission to use the family car that afternoon, to take Judy swimming, he found his world thoroughly satisfactory.

Nora's friend was coming at two; Nora would teach her to fold a crane.

"At which you are surely the resident expert," Kate said. "I hope the parents of this family kept their cool last night, after I was removed from the company. Did you?"

"Of course, dear, and didn't you like the Blanshards? I thought they were charming." Margaret sliced the cake she had baked the day before. "Not at all the way I thought they would be," she added. "Not fanatics."

"Not? Then what is a fanatic?"

"Your mother means they were good hosts; we enjoyed the evening." Mr. Thorne accepted his slice of cake and cut through it with his fork, took a bite, and leaned back contentedly. "It would be nice if everyone in the parish could enjoy today as much as I will. No receptions, no dinners, no meetings—no duties at all. A baseball game and a nap."

But not everyone did. There were some; certainly there were some. Leah spent the afternoon alphabetizing the churchwomen's list, checking each address to be sure it was up to date. She hummed while she worked; she was happy. When her father said for God's sake, did she have to do church work on Sunday, she didn't get paid for Sunday, her answer was easy.

"Aunt Grace says it must be done before September, and it's such a pretty day I don't really mind, you know."

Simon drove the red car, with the top down again, west of Bentley Falls and then north, past the end of Parsons Road. He meant to turn, but he didn't. He wouldn't force himself on them. Let Alex stew awhile. Only a week, after all. He should have kept his mouth shut, he knew that; the Lord was a gentleman, He wouldn't force Himself on anyone, what right did I have, shoving Him down their throats? Nan would call, one of these days. Or Alex would.

Or I'll do it myself. But not today. They're passing up the greatest experience in the world, and I'd probably tell them so, and then we'd be back where we began.

He drove north; he was miserable. A few miles further, however, sounds formed in his mouth, sounds of words he didn't recognize, but words, real words. He said them out loud to the wind, and he didn't understand, but knew they were words of praise and thanksgiving.

Inside the house on Parsons Road, Nancy lifted bright yellow ears of corn from the boiling water—ten minutes from garden to table—and said that Simon should come, he liked corn more than anyone.

"Simon is an ass," Alex said. "Let him buy his own corn."

"Alex, you don't mean that."

"Don't I? Did I call him when you hinted, any time you hinted this past week?"

"No, but you were busy."

"Not that busy. Look, Simon is a great guy, my good buddy, but he's not pushing his fantasies off on us." Alex surveyed the plate of steaming corn, the sliced beef, the tomatoes, and sighed happily. Here was help for a starving man. "And his timing was off," he added, helping himself to the meat. "After a long day on the beach, he's lucky I didn't tell him to go to hell."

"Brother dear, that's exactly what you did tell him."

"Did I?" He paused with his corn in midair, as though this was a startling new revelation of his character, and dropped the ear suddenly as the heat burned his fingers. "Blast! If I said it, I meant it. How to spoil the perfect day, argue religion."

"It was a good day. Kate was nice, wasn't she?" Nan watched his face as she added, "I liked her."

"Did you, Nan?" He looked pleased, she thought, but he immediately reached for the butter and laughed. "Of course you did; I did, too. A nice, sensible girl."

"Sensible?" Nan pulled the butter back to her own side of the table. "That's not a compliment, Alex. She's lovely."

"Lovely? Umm, attractive, of course, but with her mouth, too wide, and her square face—" he paused as he realized Nan was laughing at him. "All right, I noticed. Would you expect me not to notice?"

"I'd be shocked if you hadn't. But you never called her this week—did you?"

"No, but you forget. I'm her boss. I can't establish a pattern of dating the new teachers, and furthermore, Nan, I would never, absolutely never fall for a minister's daughter."

"We might have gone to church today, at least."

"Why? I enjoyed the sleep."

"But you weren't sleeping. I heard you outside, early this morning. Alexander Gore, I think you intend to be an old bachelor."

"Until I find some rich sucker to take you off my hands, that's the way it is."

"And until I find some sensible girl to take care of you, I'm stuck. Have another ear of corn, brother. You'll be eating my cooking for years, yet."

Alex took another ear and buttered it thoughtfully.

"Nan, if you want me to call Simon," he began, and she passed the platter of tomatoes, told him to shut up.

A car door slammed and he waited, his eyes on the screened door. A tall figure appeared, a wide smile breaking up the freckled face. "Ah," said Alex.

"Come in," Nancy said, and Simon stepped inside. The two men looked at each other while she held her breath, until Alex soberly shook his head.

"I knew I should have picked more corn," he said.

In the new subdivision south of town, in the white

split-level at the top of the hill, Larry Spencer waited until Isobel put dinner on the table before he spoke his mind. You couldn't talk to someone who was cooking, especially someone like Isobel, who fluttered from stove to sink to refrigerator, back and forth without stopping, gathering, mixing—it was a miracle that dinner was ever ready. And the roast. She'd ruined that expensive piece of beef, putting it in the oven before they went to church. My God, you'd think she'd know how to cook a roast. Not on Sunday.

He poked the crisp blackened outside with his fork before he sliced it, and sliced it before he spoke.

"I won't have it," he said.

"Of course not, dear." She stopped spreading her napkin, her fingers fluttered upward.

"You made me look a fool again, and I won't have it. People stared at you this morning."

"Oh, no, Larry."

"You don't kneel for half an hour when you get to church. It isn't necessary. People will think—"

"Everyone kneels, Larry. It's like saying hello to God. Everyone does."

"Not halfway through the first hymn. You said a hell of a lot more than hello."

"But—"

"And muttering through the prayers. I'll tell you, Belle, the first time you forget and start that idiotic tongues-talking out loud, I'll drag you out of church by the hair. I tell you, I won't have it!"

"Larry, I wasn't." She put her fork down, the first bite still intact upon it, and folded her hands. "I wasn't muttering. I know what's right as well as you do. I have respect for the Lord, which is more than you—"

"Don't tell me!" He stopped her with his fork, pointed across the table. "Just don't tell me!"

"You're afraid," she said. She picked up her fork again, held it in the air as though she might, eventually, eat the meat poised on its tines. "You know the Lord loves you, and you're afraid to love Him back."

"Love Him back? Does anyone do more for that church than I do? You can love the damn Lord without—"

"Larry!"

"All right." He turned his attention back to his meat and potatoes. Isobel sat with her fork in the air. "Eat, for God's sake; you'll die of malnutrition while you mutter your prayers."

"All right, Larry." But the meat stayed on the fork while Isobel stared out the window.

"Belle, listen. I try to understand, you know I do. But how come, after all these years you were happy, you didn't go off half-cocked—"

"Because I didn't know the Lord had these gifts for me, Larry."

"I don't get it." He finished his salad, catching the last piece of lettuce as it slipped up the side of the wooden bowl. "Honest, Belle, I just don't get it."

"It's because Jesus loves me, Larry."

"Well, hell, we learned that in Sunday school, didn't we? Old Mrs. Bentley used to sing that song, God, Belle, remember? Come on and clear up here, let's take the boat out. That'll get your feet on the ground." He shoved his chair out, stood up before he heard himself. Then he laughed. "Pretty good, wasn't it? Take the boat out, get your feet on the ground! Come on, hurry up."

Isobel put the fork down and listened as Larry clattered up the steps, slammed the bathroom door. Then she scraped both plates and carried them to the kitchen. If only Larry would wait until after dinner to argue; she never

could eat when he fussed at her. And he wouldn't listen—
he never did listen.

She filled the dishwasher, taking swipes at her eyes
between pieces, her mind flitting between the horror of
going back on the lake today, and the worse horror if she
refused. Larry hated it when she refused.

He thought it was all in her head, and she'd get over it.
If only he could understand that some people are not
sailors.

But Jesus does love me, He does. The dishwasher door
snapped shut and Isobel turned the knob, pushed it in
place.

"Thank You, Lord," she whispered, safe below the whirr
of the motor. "Thank You for all my blessings."

Grace Wyndham was not praying. She sat in Grandmother Wyndham's Boston rocker, in the morning room of
the half-timbered house on Riverside Avenue. Eleven
rooms, three baths, too much house for two people, three if
you counted Lillian, who slept in, now, since Walter went
to school. But what would happen to the house if she
moved? And where would the furniture go, who wanted it?
The girls had their own, neither one liked old things, yet.
Perhaps they would change. And the drive, that angled too
suddenly around the house toward the carriage house—the
garage, she ought to say, but it looked like a carriage house
even now. Yesterday Walter almost clipped the side of the
house as he came around. He must be more careful; she
must have the drive changed. Horses were one thing, they
had sense enough to go around, but cars—

She remembered how Elizabeth, her oldest daughter,
had sliced the entire bush from that corner one day. Didn't
hurt the car or Elizabeth, but Mr. Wyndham had been
furious. Furious. Mr. Wyndham insisted the drive was all

right, it was simply the driver, and of course he was right. But Mr. Wyndham, to the day he died, never drove a car around that corner. He hired a driver. He preferred to think while in a car, he said. Dear Leroy, he'd been twenty years older than Grace when they married, but always so good to her. He'd been surprised and proud when Walter was born, long after they were sure the two girls would be their family.

She looked at the bare feet hanging over the edge of the couch nearest her chair, and thought it was just as well that Mr. Wyndham never lived to see this day.

The dishwasher clicked on in the kitchen, the back door slammed; Lillian was off on her afternoon. Leaning forward in the rocker, Grace spoke to the bare feet.

"Walter, I want to talk to you. Please sit up."

The feet pulled back, a blond head appeared. Long hair tied at the back of the neck, a fuzz of hopeful beard on his chin, blue eyes that brightened a sun-tanned face—Walter looked very much as his father had looked at that age, except for the hair, of course. Stretched full length on the sofa, the bare feet now hanging over the other end, he smiled at his mother. He had a beautiful smile; she would never tell him that.

"It is very nice, having you at home," she began, choosing her words with great care. She must not break communications with this boy, that was vital.

"Except that you wish I'd go away?"

"Indeed I do not. It would be nice, however, if you tried to look the way a Wyndham should. That hair, you know, would shock your father. Your bare feet— You do have shoes, Walter? You haven't lost them?"

"Right here on the floor. But it isn't the shoes or the hair, mother. Be honest now. Last spring my hair was this long, almost. You never said a word. I went without shoes, you didn't notice."

Grace brushed an imaginary wrinkle from her navy knit. "You didn't need a ribbon last spring."

"True. Getting nice and long, isn't it?" He reached back to pat his pigtail fondly. As he leaned forward again the cross he wore fell over the sofa's arm; he rubbed the silver lovingly. Grace's fingers became fists.

"You did not wear jewelry then," she said.

"You forget, I wore a peace symbol. Now I've found a better kind of peace, I wear His symbol."

"Walter, it's peculiar—"

"Mother, it isn't. If you would let me tell you about it—"

"I don't want to hear. You think because you've discovered Jesus—why, child, we learned about Jesus when we were small. So, I thought, did you. I don't see why this is a miracle."

"But you didn't meet Him! You didn't let His Spirit fall on you, mother. You never accepted His gifts. Let me tell you about the Baptism."

"You were baptized when you were three weeks old, Walter. 'I believe in one baptism,' Walter, remember?"

"Mother, the Baptism in the Holy Spirit is not at all the same thing. It's an experience you can't wholly understand until you have it yourself, but—"

"Walter, I do not want to hear about it."

He looked disappointed. Then joy flashed back into his eyes, and he rested his chin on the sofa's arm, grinned at her.

"Very good, mother."

"The point I want to make, Walter, is that you will be going back to the University next month, and you can't spend your father's hard-earned money, unless you plan to study. Your grades this summer—" she shook her head.

"Weren't so hot, were they?" He rubbed the silver cross

against his cheek, smiling. "They'll be better again. I should never have gone to summer school, even first term. I was sick of studying. But after a month at home—by the way, mother, it's grandfather's hard-earned money, not father's. You forget."

"I don't forget. If your father had lacked a good business head, that money might be long gone. Walter, if I died tomorrow, you would be the head of this family, and you have no idea of the value of money, or how to care for it!"

"True." He stretched his arms and let them flop. "But no matter. If you died tomorrow, I'd give the girls their share and—you remember the rich young man, mother?"

"Which rich young man?"

"In the Bible. He couldn't bring himself to give it all away. I've always wanted to change the end of that story."

"Walter, you wouldn't!" Splotches of red appeared in her plump face as she leaned forward anxiously.

"Wouldn't I? Listen, Jesus said that was the only way for the rich man to enter the Kingdom of Heaven. And I want in, mother, praise God!"

"Walter!"

"Mother, don't you love Jesus?" He rolled off the sofa, came toward her on his knees, laughing. "He's so wonderful, and He died for us, we're saved by His blood! The blood of Jesus, praise the Lord!"

Grace drew tall in her chair, she sniffed once. "Walter, we must come to an understanding. I will not listen to that kind of talk. Religion is a private thing."

"Why?"

"Because it is. It has always been. You will not talk like that in my home. You sound worse than Simon Garcia, or the Blan—"

"Has Simon found the Lord?" Walter sat back on his heels and Grace stood up quickly, pushing him away.

"I will not have it, Walter. If you live in this house for the next month, you will be civilized, you will wear shoes, and you will not praise the Lord. My son will not go around talking like some hillbilly preacher, not in this house!" She stumbled, caught herself, and held the wall. "I believe I am getting a headache, Walter. I'm going to lie down."

Walter, still sitting back on his heels, smiled gently at her. "The Lord doesn't want you to have a headache, mother. Will you let me pray for you?"

"And why do you think He doesn't? It must be part of my punishment, these headaches, though what I have ever done to be punished for—" she shook her head and rushed from the room.

Walter sat placidly a moment longer, then kicked his shoes to a neater position under the sofa, pulled a Testament from his pocket and went out. He would read about wearing the armor of God. He'd need that armor, living with his mother another month. And then, he thought, the way St. Paul said, "Having done all, I shall stand."

The Blanshards drove along the interstate, headed for an afternoon visit with their middle son and his family. They discussed the Thornes, feeling hopeful.

"John is open," Craig said.

"And Margaret is, now. She was fearful at first, but by the time they went home last night, she was all right. Wouldn't it be a blessing, if the minister and his wife . . ."

"God is moving in Bentley Falls, Chris. But Kate is a horse of a different color."

"For a chemist, you use strange metaphors, dear. Kate is bitter; her mother told me a little about that last night. We must let the Lord lead, and perhaps in time . . ." They smiled at each other.

Martin spent the afternoon smoking his pipe and reading the paper from the first page to the last, grumbling to himself about each reported item. When four o'clock came, he strolled the two blocks to Christ Church, tried all the doors, and walked around it once. He pulled three weeds from the zinnias by the office door, paused to pick the dead blooms from the dahlias along the fence, and then strolled slowly home. The church was in order. Naturally.

Chapter Ten

UNEXPECTED GUESTS from their old parish gave Kate the excuse she wanted for the next Friday night. Simon accepted her apologies, and insisted she promise for the following week. She did. She could find no real excuse and, as she told Margaret when the day arrived, she was a rotten liar.

"But I'm too tired. I've had teachers' meetings for two days. I'm beat," she said, and received no sympathy. "School starts on Tuesday. I should rest."

Margaret threaded a needle with black darning cotton and told her to wear something pretty.

"That's another thing, what *does* one wear?"

"Clothes would be decent." Pete came into the room and flopped onto the couch. "What's the crisis?"

"Me, and that prayer meeting.

"I wouldn't worry. Judy says they hardly ever hang from

the chandeliers," Pete said, and howled with laughter at Kate's shocked expression. "That's what she said, offered to take me and see."

"You don't mean Judy Lawson goes to those charismatic prayer meetings? That child?"

"Sure, she says it's neat. But she doesn't always go, tonight for instance she's going with me. She says a lot of kids show up, though. It can't be all bad."

"Your logic eludes me, brother. You mean if teenagers approve something, it must be all right?"

"Certainly." His attention was diverted by Nora, who sat on the floor beyond the sofa, cutting old Christmas wrapping paper into squares.

"Honestly, Nora, you must have three hundred cranes by now, and a new friend too. Enough is enough!" Kate sat down beside Pete; Nora kept on cutting.

"You could be reading," Margaret suggested.

"Or loafing. Don't you know school starts next week?" Pete stretched and sighed.

"I know, and that's why." Nora stacked the squares neatly. "Do you realize I have to face all new people? Hundreds of them? And I don't have anywhere near a thousand cranes."

"That's superstition and you know it." Margaret spoke sharply; Nora looked surprised.

"Of course I know it. But it makes me feel as if I'm doing something, don't you see?"

"Listen, if word leaks out that you're making paper birds, you won't *see* the school. The little men in the white coats will be after you. Bird-girl of Bentley Falls—wow!" Pete made circles with his hands; Nora laughed.

"You collect your birds, I'll collect mine," she said.

"Nice talk! Listen, birdbrain—"

Kate pushed him off the sofa and sat on him.

"Women, always stick together! Mother—" He yelled the last word, relaxed a second and caught Kate off guard, tossed her away. "Never mind, mother," he said, sitting up and grinning. "You're a woman, too."

Kate solved the problem of what to wear with a pantsuit, the better to hang from the chandeliers with, she told Margaret.

"Don't make up your mind before you get there, Kate. You look lovely in blue."

"Thank you, and I've already made up my mind, such as it is. I never wanted to go in the first place." The doorbell rang, she heard Simon talking to John, his laughter and his deep voice. "Praise God," he said, and Kate shuddered.

She saw the silver cross first, hanging at eye level as they walked in the door. Kate's glance traveled quickly up the leather thong. It couldn't be the same cross—there were thousands of them, no doubt—but it was. Kate watched, fascinated, as the young man finished putting a new bulb in place in the entrance way ceiling, jumped from the stool, and planted a kiss on the small white-haired lady watching him.

"There you are, all done," he said, adding a hug that took her feet off the floor. "Any more difficult jobs— Simon!" He whirled around, grabbed Simon's hand. "I hoped you'd be here, praise the Lord! Mother said something that made me think—"

"Nothing nice, I'm sure?"

"Definitely not. But—" his eyes reached Kate. They were troubled for a moment, then his face lit with joy, and he caught her hands in his. "You're here! The Lord is very good, isn't He? I prayed that He would seek you out."

"Easy, Walter. You come on too strong." Simon put a

hand on the younger man's shoulder. "Kate, this is Walter Wyndham, but I take it you've met before?"

"Not really," Kate said. This was a coincidence she could have lived without.

"She trampled me, isn't that an introduction? Stepped on my feet."

Kate looked quickly at his feet—ah. He wore shoes, if sandals could be called shoes. Expensive but very tired sandals.

"Kate, this is our hostess, Camilla Frey."

She saw the eyes first, dark brown eyes. Then the small-boned, pink-cheeked face and pure white hair, short and brushed back.

"You're beautiful," Kate said, unable not to say it.

"Simon, be sure she comes often!" Camilla leaned forward, brushed her lips lightly against Kate's cheek, and turned to greet the people coming in behind her. Simon led Kate to the living room, already filled with people.

"There are places on the other side," he said, but she refused to squeeze past. "Coward," he whispered, teasing, and led her through the hallway, the kitchen, and into the dining room, where they found some empty chairs.

"She *is* beautiful," Kate said, still thinking about Camilla. Simon agreed.

"About two years ago, she made up her mind she was old and worn out. She negotiated to sell this house and move into a nursing home, gave up all her clubs and her Sunday school class, and then Craig talked her into coming to a prayer meeting one Friday night. They met one day, quite accidentally—"

"Oh, no, never accidentally," Kate said, her eyes gleaming as she teased.

"Right. The Lord led Craig to Camilla as sure as we're sitting here together. And Camilla opened her heart to the

Lord, received the Baptism, and grows younger each day. She's back teaching at church, leading more groups than ever before; when they call us born-again Christians, they aren't kidding."

He introduced her to the people close by, in front of them, and she had time to look at the crowded living room, study the faces. Several young people sat on the floor in the center of the room, and others gave up their seats as people continued to arrive. It was, she decided, very sad.

"No wild eyes among them," she whispered to Simon. "They might be lifted whole from a shopping center, or a movie, or the Christ Church congregation. They ought to look different!"

"You expected halos?"

"Of course, and bumps where the wings would grow."

Simon, under the cover of the conversations around them, said he knew now why his back had been itching lately.

"But they are different, Kate," he whispered. "See the couple in brown, across the room? Behind Walter? She's wearing a pink scarf. They were read out of their church, two weeks ago."

"Read out?" Kate thought suddenly of the Bishop.

"Literally that, so help me. The minister asked them to stand during the service, and one of the other members read something—by-laws? I don't know. The point was they were no longer welcome to worship there."

Kate swallowed uncomfortably. Read out of the church? The Bishop couldn't expect—Kate could no more imagine her father being that cruel than she could imagine the miracles the Blanshards told of being true. Her fingers tightened on each other; she wished the meeting was over.

A man in a green and white striped shirt turned around

and gave Kate a songsheet, just as a clear voice across the room began singing. "His name is wonderful—"

"Number five," the man whispered. Kate found the place.

If this was a prayer meeting, she could live through it. The tunes were simple, the lyrics simple-minded. Some words came right from the Bible, she thought, set to music, and those were rather nice.

Several arms went up in the air, as Walter's had that day on the dormitory steps, almost as though they expected to catch something—or Someone.

After one slow-moving song, the room grew still, a bass voice said, "Praise God," and a murmur of many voices began. Not more than a murmur, but she realized they were praying, each in his own way. Simon sat with his freckled face lifted, his eyes closed, his lips moving soundlessly. Occasionally a voice spoke out loud. "Praise His name," "Thank You, Father." "Thank You, Jesus." Then a man's voice—Kate sat forward and identified him as one in a short-sleeved blue shirt, middle-aged.

"Heavenly Father, we gather here praising You and loving You. We thank You for all the blessings You have given us freely, Lord, and we thank You for this fellowship. We come in the name of Your Son, our Lord, Jesus Christ."

"Yes, Lord Jesus."

"—who said that if two or three were gathered together in His name—"

"Praise the Lord!"

"—and we lift up to You all the people in this group, the ones who are here and the ones who, for reasons unknown to us, cannot be here."

"Yes, Lord."

Another voice took up the prayer, a man's voice from the front hall.

"We pray, Lord, for the governor of this state, and the president of our country, and for all those in authority, that they may be led in Your way. That they may have wisdom and strength to do Your will."

"Oh, yes, Lord. Thank You, Jesus."

Kate gave up trying to tell which person spoke. When one stopped, another began; they prayed for everything under the sun and moon and stars, she thought, as her feet began to itch. Listen, Lord, if You really are, You'd better be listening, because these people believe in You. They think You are here in the midst of them.

The top of her right foot began to itch; she rubbed her left heel on it, hard.

A young girl spoke, from the center of the living room. She wore a long, red dress; blond hair fell around her shoulders. She hugged her knees as she prayed, her face lifted.

"Lord Jesus, I pray for my mother and dad tonight. I just ask Your help, because they don't understand. They are afraid of You, Lord, and afraid of this meeting, and I just ask You to touch them, Lord—"

Kate recognized Walter's voice in the loud, "Yes, Lord," that followed.

Green striped shirt in front spoke next, his voice a harsh contrast to the girl's soft one. "Lord, thank You for fixing my backache last week, I couldn't have made it without You, Lord."

"Heavenly Father—" Kate pushed against Simon, trying to see around the corner. Yes, it was Craig Blanshard speaking now, and she saw Chris beside him. "In our community, many people seek a closer walk with You, Lord. Give us the strength and inspiration to be better witnesses for You, through us open those hearts to the reality of Your Holy Spirit. We ask this in Christ's name, and we thank You, Father. We thank You."

"We praise His Holy Name."

"Thank You, Jesus, thank You."

"Listen, thank You Lord, for curing my headache this afternoon. I thought I'd die for sure, so thank You."

"—and my uncle, he's got that bad back again, Lord, and he don't believe You can heal it, but I know You can. I believe, Lord, and I claim that healing for him."

"Amen."

"In the name of Jesus!"

Kate took a surreptitious look at her watch—could it possibly be only a little after nine? The prayer was getting silly, bad backs and headaches, indeed. How about itches? If she scratched every place she itched right now, she'd look like a monkey. Even the top of her head itched.

The blond girl in red leaned back, still holding her knees, and began to sing.

"Praise the Lord, praise the Lord—" The tune was familiar. Kate's brow wrinkled until she identified it as coming from *The Sound of Music*, and they simply repeated the phrase over and over, inserting "Hallelujah" when the three words didn't fit. Kate sang along softly, as they repeated the tune again and then again, until she realized the others were no longer singing the words with which they began. Each sang different words now, or perhaps not words, perhaps just sounds—oh. Kate sat back, her eyes wide open. They were surely singing in tongues. How odd—

"Singing in the Spirit," Simon whispered.

The melody changed. For a moment it was like an orchestra, tuning up, and Kate repressed a smile. Then the various tunes melted together, harmonized, and finally, slowly, died away.

In the almost breathless silence after, a woman's voice spoke, from the dining room behind Kate.

"La ca tia, la ca pa tiah." Strange syllables, surely not words? "Lade ah ca, pa la tiah, fodio ca de oh." The voice went on, and Kate willed herself not to turn around and not to smile. Finally it stopped. The silence then had a tenseness to it, it seemed to Kate that the whole room held its breath, waiting.

"Your praises, My children—" a soft male voice from the other side of the living room began and paused, then continued as though he picked each phrase from a box. "Your words are precious to Me, My children. I have heard each one. Do not fear to believe, My children. Do not be afraid. I love you. I am the Lord."

There was a long, breathless pause after the last statement, and then the familiar answers:

"Praise God!"

"Thank You, Father."

The tension broke. People visibly relaxed, smiled at their neighbors.

A slight, dark-haired girl in blue shorts, sitting between Walter and the girl in red, waved her hand in the air, smiling. "Listen, you wouldn't believe what happened at the coffeehouse Monday night."

True, Kate thought. I probably won't believe.

"You know how noisy the coffeehouse is. Well, you don't, I suppose, but it is noisy and filled with smoke, and people talking and singing, and we went hoping to witness." She paused to take a breath. "Well, Monday night, the Lord told us—I mean, we felt we should wait on the steps outside. And we did."

"Coffeehouse is at First Church," Simon whispered.

"Well, we sat there, and the Lord sent three kids out. We witnessed to all of them and they were ready! They were open. In fact," she grinned and looked around her, "two of them are right here with us, and they like it."

"Praise God!"

"Thank You, Lord."

"Wait a minute, Jeannie, how'd you lose the third one?"

"Well, he already had a date for tonight." She flashed a smile at the teasing questioner, a gray-haired, plump man in a rocking chair. "But we'll get him here, just wait."

Blue shirt leaned forward and spoke to the newcomers. "Have you accepted Jesus as your Savior?" he asked. There was a flurry of assent, and he smiled. "We'll pray with you," he said. "If you confess with thy mouth the Lord Jesus—"

"Oh, I'm late, I'm late!"

The white rabbit, Kate thought, but it wasn't. Isobel Spencer fluttered through the crowd by the front door, pushed in and sat on the floor in the center of the room.

"Larry was supposed to be home tonight, he said he would be home tonight, but a few minutes ago he called and said he wouldn't be home until morning, so I hurried—" she looked around the group. They were listening, smiling, and accepting her, Kate thought. "Have I missed just everything?"

"Of course not. We're glad you came." The old man in the rocking chair answered her agitated question. "This is a very special evening, because we have some young people to pray through."

Kate looked at Simon, her brow raised. Pray through?

"He means pray for them, the laying on of hands, for their Baptism in the Spirit. You'll be interested, Kate."

"Not very damn likely," she thought, and the words made her feel better. "Which goes to show You, Lord, if You're still here, that I'm not ready for You."

"Time for the glory seat," Simon suggested and lifting

his own folding chair over heads, placed it in the center of the room. The woman in brown sat down, and the others gathered around, placing hands on her. Some reached through the crowd and touched her with one hand, while they lifted the other high in the air, as though this made a clear passage for the Holy Spirit. They prayed softly in tongues, and then one voice lifted in understandable prayer, asking for her peace of mind, and that she be able to forgive the minister and congregation of her former church.

When she stood up, her eyes moist and her smile joyous, another took her place on the chair. Two more were prayed for, and finally the man in blue asked if others had needs.

"No more?" He looked around, and Kate saw his eyes widen. "Isobel?"

"No, not me." Tears streamed down her face; she made no attempt to stop them.

"Come along, everyone likes the glory seat," Simon said, and reached with his big hands to lift her up.

"No, no, no, no . . ." The thin voice rose into a scream before she covered her face with both hands and huddled into a wretched heap on the floor.

Simon glanced at Kate. For a moment exasperation flared in his eyes, and just as quickly the smile came back. He patted Isobel's head, and said it was all right, she could stay right there.

Miss Frey announced that coffee was ready, and the crowd drifted onto the screened back porch, or through to the backyard, where lights revealed a swing and several chairs. Kate watched as Craig closed the wide doors between the living and dining rooms.

Simon led Kate to the porch, brought coffee and excused himself, said he would be right back. "Walter?"

That young man came over, smiling.

"Can I help?"

"You can take care of Kate for me. I'll be back in a minute."

"Be my great pleasure," he said, with an elegant bow that brought a reluctant giggle from Kate. Simon went through the kitchen, with Craig close behind.

"What are they going to do?"

"Pray with Isobel, I should think," he said. "Naturally."

"Oh, of course—naturally." And heaven knows, Isobel needs it, Kate thought. She asked if he had been at a prayer meeting before.

"Not here at home. My mother has had other plans on Friday nights," he said, with a rueful grin. "At school we started meeting several times a week, for prayer."

"Like this?"

"Oh, I think we sing more, and pray more, but otherwise it's like this."

Kate's eyes twinkled. All she'd heard tonight was song and prayer—how could they possibly do more?

"And we have more prophecy, I guess. Did you notice the man who gave the interpretation? After the lady spoke in tongues, I mean, he gave the prophecy," he added, apparently remembering that Kate might not understand. "He interpreted, you know—it takes guts to do that. You hope the words are from the Lord, but—"

"They might not be?"

"I'm always afraid they're just old Walter, getting his licks in. I don't speak up very often. But I hear the words, sometimes exactly the same words someone else has nerve enough to say. But I get scared, Miss Kate."

"Just Kate, please. You make me feel ancient. And if your mother is Grace Wyndham, I'm sure we'll meet again."

"Will we? Why?"

"My father is the Reverend John Thorne."

"The new rector?" Walter looked startled. "My gosh, Miss Thorne—Kate, I mean—does he know you're here?"

"Yes, indeed. He is even now on his knees praying for the safety of my soul."

Walter looked uncertainly at Kate, but was saved from reacting by the blond girl in the red skirt who caught his arm, excused him to Kate, and drew him away all in one quick breath. Kate watched them go and then, before anyone else came to talk, she slipped into the kitchen and around by the front hall to the living room door.

Isobel still crouched in the center of the room. Three men hovered over her—the three witches of Macbeth? *By the pricking of my thumbs, something wicked this way comes—*

With a quick movement, Simon lifted Isobel, put her on the couch, and straightened her dress, as though she were a doll some child had left on the floor.

"Isobel?" He pulled at her fingers, and she peered up at him. Sitting beside her, he claimed one thin hand and held it between his large ones. "Praise God," he said, in a soft voice.

A shudder went through her slight body. "Long ago he loved to take care of me," she whispered. "He called me his little dear."

Simon looked at the other men, his thick red brows lifted, questioning. They drew chairs close and sat in front of Isobel.

"He thought it was cute that I was afraid of his horse, or his big dogs, or—" she shivered—"or the water."

Tears slid down her cheeks. The man in the blue shirt pulled out a white handkerchief and patted her chin.

"Larry, you mean?" he asked.

"Now he thinks I'm silly."

"Isobel—"

"He makes me go in the boat, and I get so sick." She covered her face again. "I get sick," she whimpered.

"Have you prayed about that? Have you asked the Lord to cure your seasickness?" Simon questioned her gently.

"I pray for Larry every day, but I think the Lord doesn't really know."

"He knows, Isobel. Let us pray with you. You don't have to be afraid, or be sick, for by His stripes we are healed, you know that," Simon said.

"We'll stand on the blood of Jesus," Craig said.

Isobel whimpered again, and Kate backed away, pressing her spine against the hallway wall, her own stomach in turmoil. Isobel needs a doctor, not a prayer, she thought. The woman's possessed by fear, and all they can do is pray!

Chapter Eleven

"WHO WAS IT said he admired the faith, but found many of the faithful intolerable?" asked Kate, coming into the dining room the next morning.

"Any number of people, I should think, at least half of them clergymen." John Thorne folded his newspaper and put it on the table, knocking three pink zinnias from the centerpiece. "Are you describing yourself?"

"Yes—I think so." Kate retrieved the zinnias and poked one back in place. "I admired—oh, I suppose I even envied them their faith, at first. When I wasn't embarrassed for them. But—" her left brow went up, she made an impatient face, and sat down. Putting a slice of bread in the nearest side of the toaster, she watched it slide out of sight.

Margaret poured her a cup of coffee.

"The thing is, they play at being God." Twisting the

stems of the two zinnias together, Kate looked defiantly at her father. "They do—they think they have the power and the glory. They ask for miracles, if you please, and know they will happen. Or so they say."

John's smile played about his lips and settled there. "I don't think they believe the power is in themselves, Kate. You don't think that, either."

"You ought to go and listen for yourselves. You'd think they didn't know about doctors, about psychiatrists. They'll fix someone up real good some day, playing around the way they do. Poor Isobel."

"Mrs. Spencer?"

"The very same. She's a neurotic mess, and they prayed for her. Well, God knows I hope He'll cure her, but—honestly—they prayed that she would never get seasick again, as a sign for her husband, I guess."

"That's a prayer I hope God will honor," John said. "Her husband is determined that she'll go out on the lake with him whenever he wants to go, you know."

"But dad—" Kate sighed and looked down at the two mangled stems, grinned shamefacedly at Margaret. "Ruined your posies, mother."

"It doesn't matter. We have a hundred more in the yard. Kate, don't let it upset you. Eat your breakfast. Your toast—"

"Not upset me? If I had a terrible pain in my back, wouldn't you call a doctor? Wouldn't you?" She yanked the toast out of the toaster and spread butter quickly. "There were over forty people there, and Simon says that's only a small part of the potential. Simon says there are well over a hundred who might show up at one meeting, but luckily don't, since no house could hold them all. Simon says that more are becoming aware of the movement, more receiving the Baptism every week, and that's right here in Bentley Falls. Multiply that by the cities in all fifty states, and you get—"

"My turn," Margaret said, smiling. "You forgot to say, 'Simon says.'"

"Oh, mother—"

"He is a nice young man, isn't he?"

"Sometimes I think so. Only sometimes, mind you. I'm having dinner with him tonight." She took a spoonful of strawberry jam and dropped it in the center of her toast. "If he will just keep his mind on me, and not on God, for a change. Dear Father in heaven—"

"But Kate, just a few weeks ago you told me you didn't believe there was a Father in heaven."

"Touché, mama." Kate grinned. Holding the toast in front of her, as though it might keep her parents from seeing her face, she added that she'd had a thought or two about that.

"Last night, after Simon left and I went to bed, I argued with myself for hours. At least—I thought I argued with myself. Finally I realized I was arguing with God. Does that make sense? I guess if I can argue with Him, He must exist." She bit into her toast and jam, chewed it thoughtfully and then added, "I know He is."

The wind blew the curtains into the room; the coffeepot gurgled quietly. John, with a mischievous grin, remarked that he'd said it the other day.

"I can't argue with personal revelation," he said.

Kate's dimple went in, her eyes sparkled. She felt as though—no matter what else happened last night—something of great importance had been settled, and she had settled it.

Taking her coffee to the backyard and the bench there,

she thought about her discovery. She remembered glancing at the clock; three in the morning and she was still arguing with herself about what she'd seen that night. How could they expect God to heal their aching backs? In the name of Jesus, they claimed healing for split fingernails—

You miserable, puling adolescent, why shouldn't they pray for split fingernails? Or for anything else?

Puling adolescent. Those words had brought Kate's eyes wide open in the dark. She'd never used the word *puling* in her life.

"Hey, Kate!" Simon climbed from the red car in the parking lot, stepped over the low fence and came toward her, smiling. He wore white shorts and shirt, his red head gleamed in the sunlight, and he looked more Irish than ever.

"Tennis, anyone?" Kate asked, laughing up at him. He sank into the green and white aluminum chair and said no, he thanked her very much, but he'd had enough tennis today. "Already?"

"Already." He dropped his arms, his big hands sweeping the grass. "That Alex Gore plays a mean game on Saturdays. Listen, Kate, I invited Alex and Nan to go along tonight, is that all right?"

"That's wonderful." Relief must have shown in her eyes; Simon laughed and accused her of being afraid.

"Don't want to be alone with me?"

"Darned right I don't. Me and a Spanish-Irish Jesus freak?"

"Ah, Kate." He leaned back, smiling lazily at her, and she thought again that he was the most attractive man to come her way in many a long day. The light red hair on his arms and legs, the freckles on his face added to the maleness of him. Even the sweat on his forehead.

"Alex was afraid you'd be sick of him, after the teachers' meetings this week," he said.

"I didn't think he knew I was there. I do get the impression that Alex doesn't care to socialize with a faculty member. I'm surprised he'll come tonight."

"This isn't the nineteenth century." Simon frowned, and Kate could not resist teasing.

"More like the first century, don't you think? Last night?"

Simon chuckled and said, "Praise God," as though the first century would suit him fine. He told her they would pick her up about seven, and gathered himself into a position to stand as a long blue wagon pulled up beside his car, and Isobel got out.

She wore white shorts and shirt, too, with white boating sneakers and a bright orange scarf tied around her dark hair. Holding a package in front of her, she stepped over the fence and came toward them, smiling.

"Don't get up, Simon, I'm just bringing this to the house— Hello, Kate. My you look pretty today, doesn't she, Simon?"

She paused almost long enough for Simon to agree, and talked on. The day was so absolutely lovely, and she'd felt so good that morning, she'd jumped out of bed and hurried downstairs to bake some cakes for the weekend, and some banana bread. She'd brought a loaf of that for the rectory family. That darling Nora and Pete, she knew they'd enjoy her banana bread.

"We're going sailing this afternoon, you know," she said, and when Kate showed alarm, she patted her arm and said she shouldn't worry. "I feel just wonderful, and I know I'll have a perfect day on the lake. I'm not afraid anymore, Kate. Larry will be surprised, won't he? I'll never be seasick again, I just know that. I know that."

Fluttering her fingers at them, she hurried toward the back door, taking dainty, sneakered steps across the grass.

Kate closed her eyes.

"She'll be all right," Simon said, reaching out to touch Kate. "Don't worry, she'll be fine."

"How can you know? How can she be so sure, all of a sudden she's invulnerable."

"She knows, Kate. She knows God won't let her down."

Tears stung at Kate's eyelids. She blinked them back quickly. "Sometimes God has ideas of His own," she said.

Chapter Twelve

MR. THORNE went to the parish house at eleven for a very short meeting and asked Kate to follow soon after, and type up some notes for him. At the office door she heard a shrill nervous giggle, an angry voice, and her father's soothing tones. She walked on to the hall entrance. In the outer office, Leah was happily inserting blue fliers into the Sunday bulletins.

She wore her usual high-necked blouse, a pink flowered one this morning. Her hair was pulled back by the usual elastic, but some had escaped and danced around her face as she worked.

"Good morning!" Kate stepped in with a cheerful smile. "The sound and the furies seem to be meeting with dad. May I help you while I wait?"

"The sound and the furies? Oh—" Leah giggled and stopped working, a blue flier held in midair. "You needn't help, Miss Th—Kate. They won't be too long, I shouldn't think. Aunt Grace said—"

"Is Mrs. Wyndham there?"

"My goodness, of course. It's the Altar Guild nominating committee. Aunt Grace says Helen ought to be elected directress again, if she wants to be."

"Helen Bentley?" Kate had never met Miss Bentley, the last of that family to stay in Bentley Falls, but she knew her by sight, a slender spinster with a vast pile of dried-weed-colored hair. "Does she want to be elected?"

"She says not. She always says not. But she'll be mad if she's not elected, you'll see. I may be wrong, but that's what I think, and Aunt Grace does, too."

"Then you aren't wrong." Kate sat down at the table. "Miss Bentley shouldn't say she doesn't want something if she really does."

"Shouldn't she?" Leah looked surprised. "No, of course she ought not, but Helen is just like that, you know." She stopped work again, adding, "Of course you don't know, do you?"

"Not yet, but I'm learning," Kate said. "Where can I get a really good haircut in Bentley Falls, Leah?"

"Oh, my goodness, let me see." Leah not only stopped work now, she sat down. "Well—oh, of course. Aunt Grace goes to Anthony's, on First Street."

"But can he cut hair? I mean really well?" Kate pressed Leah to think for herself, but Leah was ready.

"Aunt Grace wouldn't go there unless it was best," she said.

Kate thought about Mrs. Wyndham's graying, permanent curls, which did exactly nothing for her plump face, and decided to ask Nan about a good shop. "That's a pretty blouse, Leah," she said.

"Thank you." When Leah blushed she was suddenly pretty. Kate felt a rush of sympathy for her.

"Leah!" At the voice of Aunt Grace, her niece turned quickly. "Leah, the ladies say you are too busy to order the flowers for us. I said that was nonsense. Why in the world shouldn't you do it? You're right here." Mrs. Wyndham sailed across the room as she spoke and stood close to Leah. "Good morning, Miss Thorne. Now Leah, you don't feel it's too much, do you?"

"Well, Aunt Grace, I don't know—"

"Of course you don't. I knew it. And Leah, we'll put you down for treasurer, too. You have a head for numbers." She turned to Kate. "She really does, you know. A splendid head for numbers, and the books last year were a disgrace!"

"But really, Aunt Grace—"

"There. I'll just tell the girls that's settled. You'll be the treasurer, and of course you'll order the flowers. She's my right hand, Miss Thorne. I'd be lost without Leah. She's a good steady girl."

Leah's cheeks blushed a bright pink. Her eyes followed her aunt across the room. The office door closed again and Leah sighed.

Kate watched her. The rush of sympathy she'd felt before gave place to nausea. I may vomit, she thought. That girl enjoys being walked over. Trample a little harder, Auntie, do.

"I think I'll go home and make myself useful," she said. "The meeting doesn't seem to be over."

"Oh, please don't go. We were having such a nice little chat, weren't we? And I'm almost finished. Then I won't have a thing to do. Everything's ready for tomorrow, you see, except these. I go home at noon on Saturday. There wouldn't be time to start anything else."

"It's too bad you have to come in at all on Saturday," Kate said, leaning forward to pick up blue fliers and a pile of bulletins. If their nice little chat was to continue, she wanted something to do.

"But someone has to be here. Sometimes the ladies forget their days to do flowers, you know. And the bulletins are never ready earlier. Sometimes they are, but—" Leah pushed some strands of hair from her eyes and sighed.

"I don't believe the church could get along without you either, Leah."

"Oh, no, anyone could do what I do. In fact, Aunt Grace says I'm awfully slow. But I do get things done, and she likes having me here." The phone rang, interrupting her, and Kate worked quietly while Leah went to answer. At her greeting, however, Kate came to attention. There couldn't be two named Camilla in one medium-sized church. This must be her hostess of the night before.

"Mr. Thorne hasn't mentioned the confirmation class, not yet," Leah said. "Of course the Bishop will come the second Sunday in Advent. He always comes the second Sunday in Advent. But Camilla—" Leah's posture changed now. Kate realized she was about to be diplomatic. Her voice took on a conspiratorial tone. "You know, you've had that class for several years, Camilla. I'd surely think you would like someone else to take it over, one of the other teachers, perhaps. Or—"

Apparently, Camilla didn't agree. Kate listened, amused, as Leah promised at last to tell Mr. Thorne she had called. Was it her father, or Aunt Grace, who asked Leah to talk Camilla Frey out of teaching the new confirmation class? Probably Aunt Grace, Kate thought. Almost certainly Aunt Grace.

Leah replaced the receiver with a small shrug, came back

to the table, and picked up the conversation exactly where she'd dropped it. "I don't suppose I'd want to be at home all day on Saturday anyhow," she said.

Kate thought if the rest of the family treated her as Aunt Grace did, that was understandable.

"Tell me about Walter," she said, slipping the last flier into the last bulletin.

"You needn't bother, cousin, I can do that myself."

Leah jumped and turned, quickly. Kate looked up and laughed. Walter, long hair flying, the ever-present cross shining against a blue sweatshirt, and tennis shoes that only just fulfilled the law about not driving in bare feet. He swung a chair around, straddled it, and asked what was so funny.

"You. You're an anachronism in Leah's neat office."

"Then she should change the office," he said, and asked Kate what she wanted to know. "My life's an open book, praise God."

"Walter, my goodness!" Leah held the Sunday bulletins tight against her chest and stared at her younger cousin. "You don't swear in the church building, Walter, and you ought to shave."

"Praising God is not swearing, cousin, and this—" he fondled the fuzz on his chin—"this is going to be a beard."

Leah separated the bulletins into packets and slipped rubber bands around them. As she worked, she glanced at Walter, then shook her head at Kate, as if warning that he was a terrible adolescent and likely to remain so forever.

"What was it you wanted to know about me? I've brought mother's chariot from the garage, but I see she isn't ready."

"What makes you tick, for instance?"

"The Lord," he answered promptly.

"Walter!"

"Well, praise His name, it's true, cousin. What next, Kate?"

"Walter, this is Miss Thorne. You should call her that."

"It's all right," Kate said. "I once stepped on his feet. He may call me anything he likes."

"On my *bare* feet," Walter said, adding to Leah's confusion.

"Is that why you wear shoes now?" Kate asked.

He wiggled a large left toe through a convenient hole in the canvas and said it was the civilizing influence of Bentley Falls.

"He means Aunt Grace. He talks a lot of nonsense, Kate. I wouldn't pay much attention." Leah explained that she would be right back. She must put the bulletins in place for the ushers, next morning. Walter stared out the window until the click of her heels, going up the stairway, faded. Then he looked at Kate again, his eyebrows raised.

"When do you go back to school?"

"The twenty-eighth, if I go. I'm not sure. I'm waiting on the Lord for that." He leaned against the back of the chair, his chin on his arms, and looked out the window. "I'm so new in the Lord," he said plaintively.

"But of course you'll go back to school. You're surely registered?"

"Yes, but should I? Is there some other work I should be doing?"

"Walter, that's—" Kate stopped. It wasn't her right to tell him how silly he sounded, after all. But he was listening to his own thoughts, now.

"I was a month old in the Lord, practically brand-new, that day I met you on campus. I wanted to share the Good News with everyone."

"I noticed," Kate said.

"I guess you did. But, my God—my gosh, Kate, you

didn't know me before that. You didn't know what was happening to me on that campus. I couldn't hack it."

"Classes, you mean?"

"That, and the cats in the dorm, just so darn many people, all in one place. Listen, I was lost first quarter." He stared ahead of him, seeing through Kate to the wall, his face drawn tight, looking strangely middle-aged. "I made friends though, finally, and they were like me. We found ways to forget the whole thing, you know."

"Drink or drugs?" she asked quietly.

"Drugs, of course. Liquor shall never pass these ruby lips, girl." He grinned suddenly. "You should have seen my friends. You'd think I picked them to hassle mother."

"That's a rotten reason."

"Well, I didn't just stand there and say 'Hey, that cat is far out, mother would really hate him.' I just gradually moved into a crowd that was as different from anyone in Bentley Falls as I could find. And funny thing, Kate, they're all smart guys. I mean, really intelligent. They experimented with drugs, they didn't just drown in them. We all did. And my grades went down, but I didn't much care, you see?"

Kate did see. It was a story she'd heard a hundred times in the high school where she taught before. Just an experiment. They always said that.

"This summer a bunch of us moved into an apartment, took enough class-work to keep the parents happy, and planned a great scientific study of the effects of LSD."

"Oh, Walter—"

"Yeah. Oh." He looked up at the ceiling, as though he didn't quite believe it himself. "I know I might have loused myself up for good, but I didn't admit it then. I thought I could back out if things got bad, and tell you the truth, Kate, I think all the fellows thought that. I mean, we got

~ 118 ~

the stuff, but we kept putting off the experiment—praise God! Anyhow, the Lord stepped in, and I didn't have to go on with it. On the Fourth of July. That's why I didn't stay for the second term, you see. I had to get out of that place."

"The Fourth of July? Sounds like a great scene for a movie, the road to Damascus on the Fourth of July—flags, crowds cheering—"

"And trumpets trumpeting?"

"And angels angeling," Kate offered. He laughed and said no angels.

"But there were flags. The street was lined with them when I went out that morning. I came down Fifteenth and stood at the corner and looked at all those flags. I remember thinking they stood for the greatest country in the world on the one hand, and goddamn wars on the other hand. I strolled over to the campus and stretched out on the grass in the sun, all by myself."

"And the heavens opened, lightning flashed, and a voice—"

"Listen, this isn't a joke, you know." Walter went to the window and stood flipping the venetian blinds. Kate said she was sorry. "I doubt it," he answered, but he came back, straddled the chair again.

"And then what happened?"

"Well—there was this fellow. He came along with the freakiest bunch of guys, looked like they'd all be stoned by dark, you know? They sat down near me, and he started talking to them about Jesus. I was comfortable, and I didn't want to move, but it was either move or listen. The sun was hot and I didn't want to move."

"So you listened."

"Right. He was a black cat, one of those long clean-looking guys with a white shirt on, and a clear voice that pretty soon sounded as though he was talking to me, not them at all, and I listened. It was like I'd never heard of Jesus before, the way he told it. And when he said that Jesus died for me, that His blood washed away my sin, honest Kate, for the first time I knew that meant me, too."

"I can't imagine you as a sinner, Walter, despite the drug bit. Growing up in Bentley Falls, and all."

"What does that have to do with it?" He picked a green jade, egg-shaped paperweight from Leah's desk and bounced it gently on his hand. "Bentley Falls has as much sin as any other place, girl. But the next thing this cat said was that if I believed in Jesus, His Holy Spirit would come into me and work through me, and that's what I wanted to happen. Me, Walter Wyndham, stoned every weekend, lousy grades, scared of my own mother, and without one goal to call my own—all of a sudden I knew I had to get Jesus inside of me."

Kate stopped the teasing remark she wanted to make, and waited.

"I rolled over, and I thought 'Jesus, if You want this body of mine, this soul of mine, You can have it. I haven't done much with it in the nineteen years I've had it, and if You want it, please take it. Come into me, and take over.' And He did."

"You knew that, of course, right then?" Kate kept her eyes on the green jade bouncing in Walter's hand.

"I knew it. I stretched out my arms, and I could feel the warmth coming along them, in through my fingers, up my arms, right into my heart."

"It was a hot day, last Fourth of July," she said softly.

"But this wasn't the sun. Don't you think I could tell the difference? I'd been lying in the sun, Kate, and I was hot, fine. But this was different. This was God's love coming into me and cleaning me out, see?"

"I see what my father keeps telling me. You can't argue

~ 120 ~

with personal revelation," she said. He thought about that a moment before he grinned and said it was true.

"The next thing that happened, that same night after I'd been born again in the Lord, which is fancy talk for what happened on the oval, is that I got the Baptism."

"At least I know you don't mean water on the forehead." Kate sighed. "I've learned what that means, when you people say you've got the Baptism. You mean the Holy Spirit, and speaking in tongues."

"Right. No screaming or shouting, no tears, no nothing but kneeling there, praising God, and then you begin to speak in another language. And you feel great! It's the most amazing experience, Kate. You'll never regret it."

"True. I'll never *have* to regret it. Look, Walter, about school?"

"Oh, that. I have to wait on the Lord. Listen to Him."

"Go and prepare yourself, I should think. Jesus did."

"Sure, but—" he grinned, and looked all of ten years old. "The thing is, I want to witness, and my classes could interfere."

"My father always says one must fix his priorities," Kate said. "I loathe that idea, but it is true."

"The Lord comes first, Kate. Always. That priority *is* fixed."

He stopped as the other office door opened and three ladies trooped noisily down the hall. Grace Wyndham came more slowly, stopped at the doorway.

"Well, Walter, you're here. Where is Leah?"

"Right here, Aunt Grace. I was just putting—"

"Have you sent the cards about Wednesday's Guild meeting?"

"No, but I—"

"They must go out today, Leah. I don't understand what you do with your time."

Mr. Thorne came into the room, saw Walter and went toward him, hand outstretched.

"This is my son, Walter," Grace managed to sound both motherly and disgusted. "I would apologize for his appearance, but—"

"It's Saturday, mother. I would certainly like to talk to you some day, sir."

John told him to drop in, anytime.

"I'm sure you have nothing to talk about that would interest Mr. Thorne." Grace propelled her son toward the hall.

"We both love the Lord, mother," Walter said, and Grace hurried him then, turning with a furious face to say goodbye. Kate followed her father into his office. Leah was already typing postcards, presumably those of the Altar Guild. Her hair hung about her face, her shoulders were hunched, and her eyes, as she looked up to return Kate's farewell, were wild and dark.

Chapter Thirteen

FIVE HUNDRED THIRTEEN CRANES floated near the ceiling of the pink room. When Kate went upstairs to dress late that Saturday afternoon, she looked but was not amused. The humor disappeared, she thought, about the three hundred mark.

"How can you sleep in here?" Ducking under the lines of floating birds, she dropped onto Nora's bed. "They'd give me nightmares."

"I pretend I'm at camp. You know, the breeze blowing the leaves outside the tent? It's kind of nice."

"Kind of nutty."

"I know it. But Kate—" Nora brushed long brown hair in front of her face. "Are you as scared of Tuesday as I am?"

"The first day of school? Twice as scared, probably."

"But you'll be the teacher. You'll be the boss."

"You hope," Kate said.

"Oh, you will. My sister can do anything." Nora grinned at Kate, peeking from behind the curtain of hair. Then her mouth turned down. "I'll just be one new kid in a big new school."

"But by the end of the week, you'll have friends. I may have nothing but enemies." Kate stretched out on the bed, looking up at the cranes. "Tell you what, if it gets too bad, I'll help you fold birds next weekend. Maybe they'll be lucky for me."

"No, I have to do them myself." Nora brushed her hair back. "You'll have to make your own."

"Not me." Kate groaned and closed her eyes, but opened them at once. She could not ignore five hundred cranes.

Margaret called Nora for dinner, and Kate ducked under the birds again, went through the hall and into the blue east room. She closed the door and leaned against it.

"Listen, God." She spoke softly and paused, as though waiting for Someone somewhere to turn, reluctantly, to listen. "We need Your help, Nora and I. Help her make friends quickly, and throw out these stupid birds. And help me through tonight, and then, please Lord, could we forget the charismaniacs? Could I meet some nice ordinary people, the kind who say the creed by rote?"

She closed her eyes and remembered something from the Friday night prayer meeting, something those charismatics said after every prayer. "Thank You," she whispered.

Because, Simon had explained, once you pray, you know your prayer is answered, and you say thanks.

If he was right, the outlook for the days ahead seemed brighter. Kate hurried to get dressed.

Alex came to the door for Kate. As the screen shut behind them, he said he hoped she wasn't upset about the change of plans, about their butting in. Kate stopped on the second step and looked at him; he was serious. The mole beside his eye was plainly visible.

"Alex—I do call you Alex on Saturdays, don't I? Well, look, of course I'm glad. I'm grateful. Didn't Simon tell you about the bet?" When he nodded, she added, "Simon and I are not on the same wavelength, you know."

"I'd think you would be," he said, frowning a little, and then the dark mole disappeared as he laughed. "As for that, who is? Who can understand Simon?"

They drove to the lake, because Simon said he felt like dancing, and this was the only place in miles where dancing and food were both available.

"Looks like a roller rink," Kate said, crawling out of the small car. Simon said it had been, once.

"Also a dance hall, years ago," he said. "When I was a kid, we had a cottage over there, beyond those woods, and I'd sneak over at night to watch them dance. But it's been a fairly decent place to eat for the last couple of years, and the music isn't bad. Loud, but not bad."

They were waiting for dessert when Alex asked Kate to dance. They made their way through the passages between tables and reached the open floor as the band slid into a slow and dreamy version of Stardust; Kate said that tune would never disappear, and Alex said he hoped she was right. She discovered that she fit well in the curve of his arm. They moved together as though they'd been practicing.

"Why do they call you Kate?" he asked. "Why not Kathy?"

"Because I'm a Kate sort of person, I suppose."

He laughed and held her closer and stopped talking. She closed her eyes, her cheek rested against his shoulder, and she thought he was a difficult man, one moment personal and the next the sound school man. She liked dancing with him, the feel of his arms around her, and wished that the music would go on, without stopping.

But the music stopped, and Simon signaled that their coffee and dessert waited. They went back to the table silently.

Afterward Simon suggested they go out on the balcony, before dancing again.

"You can see the lights curving around the bay, downright romantic out there," he said, and they went. The balcony was high over the beach, and they could see more than the lights across the water. There were three campfires on the beach below, and in the firelight figures dancing, rhythmic writhing, Simon said, tanned bodies moving while voices and radios made a cacophony of sound. The leaping orange fires made constantly moving frames for the figures below.

"The teenagers have taken a beachhead," Alex said.

"Notice the native clothing." Simon leaned over the railing. "The aborigines in their bikinis."

"Looks like great fun. Couldn't we join a party?"

"Sorry, Nan, we've passed the age barrier." Simon sighed. "Looks as though some have spent the summer here, check the piles of stuff they have."

"Just a day's supply," Kate told him. "You can't spend a day at the beach without a few changes—"

"Simon, look!" Nan pointed to the group directly below the balcony, where the fire shot red and yellow flames toward them, and outlined the faces around the circle. "Isn't that Walter? Right there?"

Four sets of eyes peered down. Simon agreed that it was Walter.

"And Judy Lawson with him," he said. "Doesn't seem

like their kind of fun, but with summer almost gone, why not?"

Kate thought of Pete and felt sorry for him. Walter, being older, would be tough competition.

"I think they're arguing," Nan said, leaning out. Alex shushed her.

"Listen," he urged, his face intent. "Just listen."

"Why shoot me down, man?" Walter's voice came loud and clear. "I'm telling you, it's the greatest thing in the world. Listen, let us tell you about it—"

"He's witnessing for the Lord!" Simon leaned out further, trying to hear. "What a damn fool place to try that—"

Kate clutched Alex's arm. Walter would be in trouble, trying to change those kids below, he was an absolute—

"Idiot," Alex said. "They won't listen to him, he's a damn idiot." But he leaned over the railing, too, trying to hear, watching Walter. Someone below turned the radio up and they could no longer make out the words, but it was obvious the bathing-suited kids around the fire wanted no part of Walter or Judy. They went on dancing, or necking, or staring into the flames, while Walter motioned and talked, and Judy nodded her head, adding to whatever he was saying.

"But Christ is the answer," Walter shouted, above the noise of the radios, and a tall tanned boy grabbed for Judy then, swung her into the air, and shouted about his kind of answer. As he yanked at her clothes, Walter leaped across the edge of the fire, and others leaped, too, caught Walter and threw him down, shouting. Alex tore away from Kate.

"Stay here," he shouted, and raced with Simon for the steps. Kate grabbed Nan, and together they stared at the milling, squalling bodies on the beach.

"Oh, God—I can't even see Judy now," Kate whispered, and Nan said there she was—no, it wasn't, it was another girl—there, over there, but Walter must be underneath—

The men appeared below the balcony and suddenly it was over.

Nan and Kate raced for the steps. A very battered Walter sat on the sand, his shirt torn across the back, ripped open in front, blood running down from his mouth. Judy stood near Simon, holding his arm, talking excitedly.

"It was all right," she said. "The Lord would have watched over us. We were all right."

"Maybe the Lord sent us," Simon suggested, gently.

"Yes, maybe. But Walter—" She leaned down. "I found your cross, Walter. They tore it off but I found it. Listen, everyone—" she turned toward the crowd of kids, hovering in the dark under the balcony. Judy's hair was wild, her shirt torn halfway across, but her smile was infinitely sweet as she looked at them. "Listen, we only want to tell you about something wonderful that happened to us. Won't you let us tell you?"

"Tell it in church."

"Go to hell, Baby."

They melted into the night. Simon stopped Judy from following. She looked disappointed, then her face brightened.

"We'll sit on the steps, Walter. Do get up. We'll go over by the parking lot and sit on the steps. The Lord will send kids to listen."

Walter shook his head and stood up. Alex told Kate later that half a dozen boys were on top of him, pounding, when they arrived. Probably thought we were cops, he said, the way they evaporated when we appeared. Now Walter pulled himself together, twisting his head to be sure it was still attached, flexing his shoulders and arms.

"I'll sit on the steps," he said. "You sit in the car."

"I will not!"

"You'll both go home." Simon herded them ahead of him, toward the steps leading to the parking lot. "You can't help the Lord if you're dead, Walter. And Judy shouldn't be here, at all. You need a gang to witness to this crowd."

"But we have to make fools of ourselves for the Lord sometimes," Walter protested.

"But not idiots," Simon said.

Alex took Nan and Kate back to their table. Nan went on to the ladies room and Kate sat down, staring at nothing, seeing the tumble of legs in the firelight, and the boy tearing at Judy's clothes. She shivered.

"Exactly," Alex said, his voice stern. "Get religion and lose your common sense. That's why I'd rather hoe on Sunday morning."

Kate slowly focused on Alex. "I don't see the connection," she said.

"Oh, God! Church, religion, butting in where you aren't wanted, proselyting, evangelizing—if religious people would spend half that time helping people who want help, who deserve help, God, what a world this would be! What possible good did those brats think they could do out there?" He jerked his head angrily toward the balcony and the beach.

"Those brats were not precisely working for the church you don't attend on Sundays," she said slowly. "But you can't say help isn't needed out there, Alex. Didn't you notice? All those other kids at the other campfires—what would have happened if that fight had started on the schoolground?"

"Bloody free-for-all," he said. "What's that got to do with it?"

"Well, think about the beach, Alex. There were two other fires, crowds of kids, but none of them joined in the fight, and they must have heard it. They must have noticed, and if all the kids down there had started fighting, you and Simon might have been murdered! But the others kept on dancing, dancing in the firelight."

"All stoned, you mean," he said thoughtfully, and she nodded.

"They must have been. They went on dancing in the firelight, didn't pay any attention at all . . ." Her voice drifted away as her imagination brightened the scene again. She shivered.

Chapter Fourteen

KATE DECIDED her father could exist without knowing about this particular charismatic fiasco. Walter wouldn't tell his mother, therefore Mr. Thorne didn't need to know and Kate could escape going over it, worrying about it, thinking of Alex and his reaction, his irritation, or the other young people on the beach. She hoped she could escape all that. She could wait until next week, until the holiday weekend was over and gone, before she mentioned it.

Grace discovered Walter's condition the next morning. She demanded an explanation, and for the first time since the Fourth of July. Walter used subterfuge. He said he'd been on the bottom of a pile of boys, which was certainly true. Then he added, laughing, that even touch football could be rough. Grace lectured for the full twenty minutes she spent disinfecting and bandaging him (despite his protests that Judy had already done an admirable job) and finally let him alone to rest and groan in peace.

A week later, she rushed into Mr. Thorne's study.

Judy, it seems, told no one about their unsuccessful beach ministry except Jeannie, her friend in the charismatic prayer group.

Jeannie told no one but her mother.

Her mother mentioned it, with many head-shakings, to her neighbor Mrs. Belle, who told the girls at her bridge table the following Friday. Mrs. Carruthers, dummy at the next table, listened carefully and repeated the story to her pastor.

Pastor Jeffries, on his usual Monday stroll from his house on Webster Court to his own church, stopped to meet Mr. Thorne. Standing in the hall after their friendly, get-acquainted chat, he added a word of warning.

"Listen, Thorne, some of your kids have been trying to convert the beach babies, I hear. Didn't know you went in for that sort of thing." He cleared his throat unhappily. "Young Walter Wyndham, for one. I hear he took quite a beating from a gang of them, a week ago. I shouldn't imagine Grace would like that."

And Leah, overhearing, carried the story to Aunt Grace at lunchtime.

"Trouble! I told you. I warned you that those people were nothing but trouble, and now look! What are you doing about it?" Grace stood before Mr. Thorne's desk, her plump face spotted red by her rage, her chins trembling. "And don't tell me you don't understand. I know Pastor Jeffries told you—" She stopped to sniff twice and blow her nose.

John quickly identified Leah as the tale-bearer and

made a mental note to discuss the matter of privacy with her. Outwardly, however, he was calm. He helped Mrs. Wyndman to a chair, patted her shoulder, and said he'd only heard that morning himself, and didn't understand, and wouldn't she tell him about it?

She would. Fifteen minutes later he congratulated himself on his chosen therapy. The spots of color were leaving her face, the chins had stopped quivering. She was, in fact, beginning to be coherent. And—slowly—to run down.

He decided to ignore the remarks she'd made about the evil Blanshards and the fiendish Camilla, the devil Simon Garcia or the hussy Judy Lawson, about the charismatic group in general, and the Jesus people at the University who had started it all. That left Walter, and the Lord.

"—and those terrible bruises are still visible," she said, coming full circle at last. She paused for breath and John took a chance.

"Young people today are do-ers, aren't they? They act out their beliefs."

"Do-ers!" She sputtered something about liars. He smiled and went on.

"When we were young, we lacked their drive to help others, or else suppressed it. Must make you proud of Walter."

"Proud!" She drew herself up. He easily imagined a line of ancestors peering over her shoulder, each with the same furious expression and damp blue eyes. "Proud of my son converting delinquents on the beach? Please, don't try to convince me that Walter was doing his Christian duty—he has never been permitted to mix with that sort, never."

"But Walter's getting a bit old to care about permission, isn't he? I'm sure he felt he was serving the Lord."

"I don't believe you understand my problem, Mr. Thorne. I don't believe you sympathize with it at all. You are supposed to be our spiritual adviser."

"Adviser, yes. But Walter has not accepted *me* as his Lord, he's accepted Jesus Christ. And Christ is a leader who will not harm Walter, you may be sure of that."

She stared at him. "He might have been killed," she said.

"But he wasn't."

Her lips drew into a tight, narrow line; her hands made fat fists. "He attends those secret meetings," she said bitterly.

"Secret meetings?" He sat forward, startled. This was something new. "What kind of secret meetings?"

"Those prayer meetings. I warned you about them, their magic, the so-called healings. Tongues-speaking! The only thing special about those people is that they are all insufferable! All!"

"But those meetings aren't secret, Mrs. Wyndham." He sighed his relief. *Those* meetings.

"Aren't they? Are they in the church bulletin? Does anyone talk about them in church, except in whispers?" The red spots came back around her eyes. She sniffed. "Do you know who the people are, who stay long after the rest of us have gone on Sunday morning? Who sneak off to a classroom and pray? Sneak, Mr. Thorne! They sneak. And Walter with them." She stood up, slowly drawing on her gloves, smoothing out the wrinkles. "Yesterday he came to church with me, and I waited thirty minutes in the hall. When he finally came to take me home, he explained they'd been praying for a man with an injured shoulder. He'd been healed, Walter said." She sniffed again. "Healed!"

"Did you believe him?"

"Believe him? Really!" Her eyes protruded from her splotched face; she gave one last tug to her white gloves. "He wants to pray for my headaches, says the Lord doesn't want me to have headaches. He has lost touch with reality, and what I must do, since you obviously have no answer, is to find a doctor who will understand my problem."

"Yes, that might be an answer. But let him come and talk to me first." John walked around the desk and took her arm, smiled gently at her. "Let us have a talk together."

Her expression said she was sure such a meeting would be useless. Then, as though the interview had concluded to their mutual satisfaction, she went to the door. When she turned to say goodbye, John spoke first.

"Mrs. Wyndham, let him."

"Let him?" She looked puzzled.

"Let Walter pray for your headaches," he said. Her mouth snapped shut and she went out, the click of her heels on the hall floor her only answer.

John rubbed his own forehead, wearily. He knew he hadn't helped. He should have quoted the Bible, or been unnaturally stern. He might have promised to bring the mighty arm of the established church down on Walter, or at least on his friends. Warn them of retaliation—but what kind, and for what? For loving the Lord too well?

In the midst of her first harangue, she'd mentioned the Bishop, said he would soon be here for confirmation. Should that frighten him? And the other crack she'd made, about her dear Reverend Washburn, bless his dear departed soul, he would have *done* something.

Well, he, John Thorne, wished he'd defended Walter with more vigor. He thought about his next appointment, with Larry Spencer, and wished Walter would walk in, now; he would be glad of prayer for his own aching head.

Walter did walk in, but not until eleven o'clock that night. John was thinking about going to bed; Margaret had gone already. She was tired from a day with the church-women that was, she said with an unusual touch of bitterness, a time to try a woman's soul. Thirty women with thirty different points of view about the Christmas Bazaar—heaven help the chairman.

"Try thirty different booths," John suggested, and Margaret said it might, indeed, come to that, and went upstairs.

Kate came into the kitchen wearing a short green shift in lieu of a housecoat, her brown hair brushed until it sparkled. John told her she looked approximately ten, as he poured himself a glass of milk to go with the cookies he'd found.

"I don't feel ten, I feel a hundred. And this was just the first day of the second week. Where did I ever get the idea I could teach?"

"You can," he said. "Monday is no day to evaluate—have some milk." He poured a glass for her, pushed the tin of cookies across the table, and the doorbell rang.

"Your pajamas are ducky," she said, "but the rector does not answer the door like that. I'll get it."

An oddly subdued Walter stood outside.

Kate greeted him. John, standing behind her, told him to come in.

"Looks like I oughtn't to," he said.

"Nonsense. If my pajamas bother you, I'll pull some pants on." He disappeared, and Kate drew Walter in.

When John came into the kitchen, Kate asked what the opposite of up-tight would be.

"Sag," Walter suggested, a smile hovering above his blond fringe of a beard.

"Exactly. You sag, Walter."

"Then give him some milk and cookies," John said, pulling his chair to the table again. "Best thing in the world for sag."

They talked about the weather—hot. About Bentley Falls' football team. They'd lost the opener Friday night, twelve to nothing. But hopes ran high for this week.

In the middle of a sentence telling about his experiences as lead cheerleader for the Bentley Falls team two years before—with six pretty girls and a winning season—Walter paused, and grinned.

"I guess I'm still leading cheers," he said. Kate began a smile and stopped it. "What's wrong with witnessing for the Lord, Mr. Thorne?"

John poured more milk into Walter's glass.

"From my point of view? Or your mother's?"

"Yours," Walter said.

"Nothing. I do it—at least I try to do it—every day of my life."

"Yes, sir, but that wasn't exactly what I meant."

"I know. You mean—with your witnessing. Again, nothing, as long as you use your common sense. If you want me to say you were wise to take Judy to the beach, I cannot."

"But those kids need the Lord."

"Isn't it also true that Judy was in danger?"

"We were wearing the armor of God, sir. How could she have been in any real danger?"

"Oh, her immortal soul was safe enough," John said drily, "but her physical body was not, and while we live, Walter, that counts."

"But the Lord protected us," Walter protested. "It wasn't an accident that Simon and Mr. Gore arrived, sir. You were there, Kate—"

"So I heard, finally." John growled at Kate, laughter in his eyes, and said, "The next time, young lady—"

"I didn't tell him, Walter," she explained. "Would you believe I forgot? Because of school starting, you see."

"I won't forget soon," Walter said, grimacing, moving his left shoulder gingerly. "But I still think we were right. I've been reading— Boy I really amaze myself, you know, all the books I've been reading. One guy said something like you should never pray without ploughing—"

"You could have chosen a more fertile field," John said.

They sat quietly, munching cookies, until Walter said he was sick to death of being hassled. He leaned forward, his eyes fixed on the minister's face. "Jesus is the most beautiful thing that ever happened to me. I wake up every morning praising His name. I want to tell people about the Lord."

Kate stood up quickly, patted Walter's shoulder and excused herself. John's eyes followed her down the hall; he felt oddly deserted. He smiled, however, and turning to Walter, tried to explain how people felt. How his mother felt.

"They feel threatened, you see, by the strangeness of it, especially the tongues."

"I see that, but Mr. Thorne, the tongues especially! If they only knew how great it is— In my new tongue, I've never cut anyone down, you know? I've never sworn at anyone in my new tongue. Praising God in a language completely new and clean—it's beautiful."

John said that put like that, tongues were very special, indeed.

"And not emotional. I can sit at the table and pray in tongues—in my mind, you know—while mother says grace, and she never even knows it."

John poured himself another glass of milk. Should he

chastise Walter, gently, for being impertinent to his
mother, even if she didn't know it? Or should he congratu-
late him, for living so closely in the Spirit?

Walter grinned. "You know, begging your pardon, I
don't really care about Christ Church, about the established
church, you know what I mean? But I'm worried about the
Bishop."

"Good heavens, why the Bishop?"

"He'll be here, in December?

"Yes, for confirmation. The second Sunday in Advent."

"Well, mother believes he'll do something, then— I
don't know what she expects, exactly, and it doesn't make a
lot of difference to me personally, you know, but other
people—it could make a difference to them. If mother and
the Bishop get really mad, you see. Camilla Frey and the
Blanshards, lots of people who really love Christ Church
and want to worship there. Just because they believe in
Jesus, and have faith that He can heal people, and that God
hears their prayers when they pray in His name—is that
reason enough to throw them out of the church?"

"Walter, those are the beliefs that draw people *to* the
church. It isn't because of that your mother is afraid. It's—"

"I know. The unnatural enthusiasm, the supernatural
tongues—but my gosh, religion *is* supernatural, it has to be,
any religion has to be! But she's afraid people will talk." He
twisted a saltshaker in his fingers.

"You don't know my mother. She'll have the Bishop
throw you out, too, sir—oh, you can laugh, but she could do
it. Don't underestimate my mother."

"And don't underestimate your bishop," John said.

"He's okay. I know him. He's stayed at our house a lot
of times. But he always says yes to mother, you see."

Walter crunched a cookie, chewed it, and then suddenly
shook with laughter. "It's really nutty, isn't it? Good old

Walter, always-good-for-a-laugh Wyndham, worrying about whether people get tossed out of Christ Church. Especially old people like the Blanshards."

John cleared his throat but resisted an answer. The Blanshards seemed pretty young to him. He'd be their age in a year or two. It was all a matter of perspective, after all.

"Walter, I don't know how it will work out, but the Lord knows. We'll pray that He guide us through, and we'll listen, too."

"Right now," Walter said. "Could we pray that right now? Together?"

John looked at the cookie crumbs, the empty milk glasses, and thought this was the first time anyone had asked him to pray at a cluttered kitchen table. But why not? He placed his hand on Walter's shoulder and was aware as he bent his head, resting his forehead on his hand, that Walter looked up. Walter raised his face and lifted his free hand into the air, fingers open.

"Almighty and everliving God, we are gathered in the name of Your son Jesus Christ, to ask guidance for the difficulties we are experiencing. We ask You to lead us in the right way, and to increase our understanding of You and Your will for us." John's voice drifted off. He felt as though he hadn't expressed that too well. Walter, however, nodded his head and said, "Thank You, Jesus. Praise God," and then, very quietly, he prayed in tongues.

John's eyes flew open and shut again.

"Abuna ti ah ca, oh dio loco podio, fa di a la, abuna ca ria, ti li aca, oh fasti la ti a, coo put ti ah—"

John listened closely. He'd heard Chris and Craig pray in tongues that night after their long discussion. And now Walter. Were they really from God, these strange syllables, words, whatever they were? John knew it was too fluent to be made up. He'd tried that himself in his study one day, and ended in a tangle of silly sounds. This wasn't silly.

The clear young voice went on for several moments.

"Thank You, Father," he said at last, lowered his chin, smiled at John. "Boy, I'd better get home," he said.

They walked to the door together, and Walter opened it quickly as though he was embarrassed. But it wasn't that, John thought. It was more as though he'd done what he came to do. Halfway out the door, Walter turned.

"Well, sir? Was that an emotional binge?"

"No, I'd call that real prayer, deep from the Spirit of God within you."

"Go ahead, call it that." Walter sprinted down the steps, across the lawn. He leaped for the branches of a tree, high over his head, swung there for a moment and raced on, down the street.

Chapter Fifteen

JOHN'S FIRST quiet moment the next day came at four in the afternoon, after a funeral, which came after a noon luncheon—he'd inherited his place on the Neighborhood House Committee with the job. Before the luncheon, he'd been at the hospital, where Tim Morgan, age four, was having an operation, and his mother needed her pastor to talk her through the hours of waiting.

And the trouble with a day like that, John thought, is that when a moment of quiet does come, I no longer feel like thinking. Not real thinking, enough to make sense out of the problem with the charismatic prayer group.

Charisma—a spiritual gift, a gift from God.

It begins with the Holy Spirit.

No, it actually begins, of course, long before that. It starts with each person accepting Jesus Christ as their Lord and Savior. Each member of his church did this—at least, they said they did this—at confirmation. When they renewed the vows made at their baptism. When they said, "I do." And that's about all they do say in that service. John wondered, as he wondered each time he went through a service of confirmation, how many of the new members understood what they were saying, how many really believed? Despite the long classes, held weekly for a month, sometimes two months, before the service, how many really understood? The young people were there, most of them, because their parents said they were old enough. They must be confirmed—the Protestant puberty rite—and they chose not to rebel. They went through the motions.

But supposing they meant it? Then, in the words of Isobel Spencer, they were saved. John smiled, remembering Kate's laughter as she'd repeated that first conversation to him. And then he frowned, remembering Larry Spencer earlier that week. Larry, tapping his forehead meaningfully, saying that Isobel was getting mental—it was her time of life, he supposed.

But back to charisma—once a person accepts Jesus, he is ripe for the Holy Spirit. The Holy Spirit does enter into each one of those new members at that moment, I believe that, John thought. He leaned forward, both elbows on his desk. Then why doesn't everyone speak in tongues? If tongues are a sign of the infilling of the Spirit, why not? In every Christian church across the land there comes a time when each member somehow, alone or in a group, a class, stands to claim Jesus as his Lord. Therefore, if tongues is a valid experience, a true gift available to all of us, why don't they receive it? Why don't I?

"Mr. Thorne?" Leah popped her head in the door and John looked up. "I may be wrong, but these surely aren't the right folders for next Sunday, are they? The design looks as though it's meant for Advent."

He was briefly ashamed at the surge of relief he felt, the sense of being saved from his own confusion, as he stood up and went to help Leah. She wasn't wrong, they were Advent folders; someone had goofed and mailed them early. But the church had an adequate supply of others, and between them they chose a folder appropriate for September.

"Mr. Thorne, it isn't for me to say—" Leah looked embarrassed; her eyes jumped from the stack of blue folders to John and back again. She brushed flying hair from her cheeks. "I know it isn't for me to say, but don't you think the Bishop ought to be available when people want to call him? I mean, Aunt Grace said she tried, and they said he was out of town, every time. You don't suppose—"

Mr. Thorne smiled and said he supposed the Bishop was really out of town, probably at the conference for bishops in St. Louis. It would be over on Thursday, so Aunt Grace could surely reach him on Friday. Or Saturday. Leah nodded and asked him to check the calendar before she typed it for the parish letter, and as he did this, he thought how difficult life was for Leah. Loyal above all to Aunt Grace, yet wanting him to know that trouble was brewing, preparing him. He was grateful but it was, after all, unnecessary. The Bishop would not let Grace Wyndham boss him around.

Nor, indeed, would John Thorne. But he was certain he should do something. The next two days provided fewer moments for contemplation. By Friday morning he was both exhausted and discouraged.

"John, those are your favorite eggs." Margaret waved goodbye to Nora and came back to the table. "Eat," she ordered.

"Don't you care about my waistline anymore? Poached eggs, yes, but that sauce—"

"That's how you like them, and they won't hurt you, the little you've eaten this week."

"I know, but Maggie, I must make some move, do something, and I don't know what. Here's Walter, being stupid in the name of Jesus, frightening his mother with his talk and his actions, and then Isobel with her new faith that makes Larry believe she's having menopausal problems—"

"Which could be true," Margaret said drily, pouring herself another cup of coffee.

"Oh, yes, partly. But not all. And then there is Grace herself, and her friends. Their fears are understandable, too, you know, and they need help. I don't know what my part should be, Maggie."

"John, aren't you forgetting something?"

"For instance?" He looked puzzled, and she frowned lovingly at him.

"It isn't your problem," she said. "If God is behind this movement, He will solve it for you. Turn it over to Him."

John studied the daisies on the tablecloth. "And do nothing?"

"Not necessarily. But if God wants you to do something, don't you think He will let you know? Maybe it isn't God's movement, and if it isn't—"

"My word, Gamaliel!" He slapped the table, laughing. "Naturally," he said.

"Who?"

"You, my dear. Margaret Gamaliel Thorne. Listen, could we—right now?" She said they could, and he held her hand while they sat quietly. Then, slowly, he spoke. "Most gracious and heavenly—" he paused, began again. "Lord, You know I want in every way to do Your will. I've been searching for my own answer, and that's not good. I need Your answer. So right now, this minute, I'm turning it over to You. You know all things, can do all things, and if You want me to help, just tell me so. I can't do it alone, but You can, so Lord—I lift this problem to You, in the name of Jesus." He paused again, and then added, "Amen."

"I should think so," Margaret said. Then she pointed to the rapidly cooling eggs and told John to eat. He did, declared it was the finest breakfast he'd had for days, and went to the office feeling free at last.

An hour later, he stopped writing in the middle of a sentence about poverty even here, in Bentley Falls, a sentence for his sermon on the following Sunday. He was thinking about Grace Wyndham, not poverty, and he was remembering she said Walter went to those secret meetings.

They are not secret meetings, he thought. They are open, anyone is welcome, they've even invited me. Yet she feels they are secret. Anyone not involved might feel that way. What I ought to do—

He shook his head, trying to rid himself of the odd thought, but it persisted. Closing his eyes, he thought about it more, then softly asked God if this was His idea, if it had His approval. The only answer was a feeling that this time, he was right.

Reaching for the phone book, he checked on Craig Blanshard's number at the plant, and dialed.

After that, he called the Bishop.

"I hope the conference was productive," he said, when the familiar huge voice greeted him.

"It was, John. It was. And I want you to know, the problem you have in Bentley Falls is being repeated everywhere. We aren't the only state with uprisings, John."

"Uprisings!" John Thorne laughed. "I hadn't thought of it that way. But that's why I called, wanted to tell you I've invited the ecumenical, charismatic prayer group to gather at Christ Church on Friday nights. They are having space problems, I understand, and—"

"You aren't asking my permission?"

"No, just telling you, so you'll know if our more conservative members complain."

"Very kind of you, I'm sure. You think this is a wise move?"

"Anything to get rid of the secretive aura they've acquired. I think that's essential. If it is simply another part of the church program, it will be less frightening—at least, that's my theory this morning."

The Bishop was quiet a moment, and then his laughter rolled along the wires. "I think it's worth a try, John. You may have something. Good luck."

"Thank you. If it causes trouble, I shall preach about Gamaliel first, and if that doesn't work, I'll send them all to you."

Without giving the Bishop a chance to answer that, he politely wished him well, said he would see him in Bentley Falls in December, for confirmation, and hung up. He knew that Margaret had hurried for a concordance, after he left the house, to look up Gamaliel. Now he wondered if the Bishop would do the same. Probably not. More likely he was sitting back in his chair, tapping his fingers above his comfortably large middle, trying to remember. And then he would laugh and say, "Ah, Gamaliel—keep away from those men!"

He would see John's point then. And he would agree.

One interesting development he had not shared with the Bishop, intriguing as it was. Craig Blanshard said that just last night, the men of the prayer group met and decided to ask for the use of the Christ Church parlors, because the group had outgrown the homes. And this morning, John called. Craig said the Lord was taking the lead, as usual.

John Thorne sighed. Surely he loved the Lord his God with all his heart, with all his soul and with all his mind, but in all the years of his ministry, he'd never spoken of being "led" as Craig did, never felt that personal assurance.

Jealousy was part of the problem, he thought. Grace Wyndham and her friends are afflicted by that emotion. I myself am jealous, right now. How can Craig have his close relationship to our Lord, know when He is moving in his life, while I just stumble along? Sighing, he picked up his pen and went back to the sermon.

Margaret smiled her approval, when John explained what he had done. Kate suggested sunstroke.

"I warned you, no hat in this hot, midwestern September," she said. "Now see—"

"Contrariwise, a stroke of genius," he claimed. "Not, however, my own genius. But I think it will work."

"Cause a war, you mean."

"Hopefully, prevent one. You know, Kate, turn the lights on a Halloween ghost and you have a sheet waving. Too many people are afraid of this business because they know nothing about it. They just listen to rumors. If we accept it as a normal part of the church life, list it in the bulletin as a regular meeting of the parish, albeit an ecumenical one, their fears should disappear."

"And with their fears, you hope the group will also disappear?"

"Do I?" John looked troubled. "I wonder. I'm not sure what I'm hoping, yet. If it is more than an emotional fling, if it is truly from God, we need it, Kate. Imagine a church where every Christian let himself be led by the Spirit of God. Imagine a world like that."

"I can't," she said, and she couldn't. It was beyond her ability to imagine a world like that. However, what would happen would happen, she decided. Time enough then to worry. But if Simon called, inviting her to come on Friday night, she would be too busy.

But Simon didn't call, that night or the following week, when the prayer group first met in the church parlor. On the morning after that first meeting, Kate was having breakfast with her parents when Mrs. Wyndham called.

"Yes, indeed," she heard John Thorne say. "Your idea struck me as being the very answer to our problem, Mrs. Wyndham."

Kate's eyes widened, and she looked at Margaret, who shrugged, smiling.

"But it certainly was your idea, Mrs. Wyndham. You'll recall you said they were secret meetings, and it occurred to me that—"

"Yes, indeed, these things should be out in the open. Very clever of you, I thought. Now we'll see—"

Kate shook with silent laughter— What a wicked man her father was after all. When he came back to the table, she struggled to frown.

"You, my revered parent, are a very sneaky Christian, you know that?"

"Me?" He attempted an innocent expression and failed, laughing. "Yes, I suppose so. But Mrs. Wyndham wasn't quite convinced, I'm afraid. Too intelligent by far. Tomorrow I'll preach a sermon I've been working on, one that should make even Aunt Grace understand my position. About Gamaliel."

"Who in the world was he?"

"I know that," Margaret said. "He was the one who told

the council to keep away from the Christians, to leave them alone. He said if their plan was of men, it would fail."

"Yes, but what did he do?" Kate put the coffeepot down, waiting.

"He didn't do anything, but he told the council exactly what I shall tell the congregation on Sunday morning. He said if the Christians were men of God, they couldn't be defeated."

"Oh. I suppose that's true," Kate said.

"It's true. He said the council might find themselves in the intolerable position of opposing God. Now, even Mrs. Wyndham—"

"You hope," Kate said. The idea of Grace Wyndham opposing God was not impossible, she thought. If Grace felt she was protecting Walter, or Christ Church, she'd oppose Him, all right, and even if she couldn't win, she'd make an awful mess along the way. Reaching for the bacon, she asked Nora, coming sleepily into the room, if she didn't think it would be easier to sleep without six hundred cranes fluttering over her head.

"Of course not," Nora said. "Besides, I'm the only girl at school who can fold a paper crane in thirty-three seconds."

"I'll bet you are at that," Kate said.

Chapter Sixteen

WHEN GRACE WYNDHAM announced she had a headache coming on, six out of ten times she was being truthful. She suffered terrible agonies, many days each year, and if she occasionally used that excuse to avoid a scene with Walter, she felt that was only fair. Some good had to come from the pain she experienced. Wesley Hook could discover no reasonable cause for the headaches; he was certain they were caused by her eyes. The ophthalmologist, however, invariably complimented her on the strength of those eyes, and insisted they could not possibly be at fault.

When other, deeper tests were suggested, Grace stiffened her back and her courage and said that no doubt the headaches were her cross to bear, and she would go on as before.

Sunday afternoon, following Mr. Thorne's sermon on

Gamaliel, she was in bed. She'd felt the first sharp pains while talking to the minister the day before. She'd been angry when he claimed she'd suggested allowing the prayer group to meet in her church, and she knew anger was bad for her. Two aspirins and a time of quiet, and she convinced herself that he was right, which meant she'd been right, of course, and the best thing that could happen to the prayer group was to push it into the open. Sunlight kills mold, doesn't it?

The sermon this morning reinforced her pleasure in her decision; surely the group would fail. He'd been clever about presenting his topic, had never explicitly stated that he referred to the Bentley Falls tongue-speakers, but she knew. God would never tolerate this emotional, supernatural approach to Him. He certainly could not want His followers to praise Him in every breath, to discuss Him in every conversation, and now that these people were meeting within the walls of dear Christ Church, they would find it impossible—

But, oh, her head—

She raised an arm cautiously—two o'clock, her watch said—and laid it down again. The pain, beginning again as they drove home from church—thank heavens they hadn't walked today, she would never have been able—the pain shot endlessly through her head, jagged, screeching, lightning flashes of pain. There was no safe position, even holding her whole self still, the pain kept on. She clenched her fists, and tears rolled silently down her cheeks, tears of frustration because she dared not move, tears of pain.

"Mother?"

He'd come in so silently— 'Walter, do go away."
Opening her mouth, she knew she would retch, but she did not. She must not, dared not move her head.

"God doesn't want you to be ill, mother."

~ 152 ~

"Walter." There is no dignity, hurting like this, unable to move. "Leave me alone, Walter. This is my pain, I shall bear it."

"Don't talk," he said softly. She felt his cool fingers on her forehead, wanted to brush them off but dared not move so much. She heard his voice but was afraid to scream at him, fearful of the pain.

"Heavenly Father, please help my mother. We know that You don't want us to suffer pain, and You said that we should ask for healing in Jesus' name. Therefore, in the name of Jesus, and because by His stripes we are healed, I claim this release from pain for her." He paused and Grace opened her mouth but dared not speak, as a streak of pain shot down the back of her head, another flashed across her eyes. "Thank You, Father," he said. "Thank You."

He was silent. If he prays in tongues, I shall scream, she thought. I'll rise up and—but he did not. She knew when he lifted his hand. The warmth was gone, but she could not open her eyes. The brightness, even in the darkened room, would be too much. If she could only sleep!

Hearing the door close, her eyes automatically opened and shut again, quickly, afraid. Then, cautiously, she opened them wide. No arrow of fire crossed her lids. I've been asleep, she thought. I've slept and the headache has gone. Thank heavens! Sleep that ravels up the sleeve—no, that isn't right. She smiled and was grateful that small movement did not hurt. It was safe to smile. Sleep that knits the raveled sleeve—that's better.

I must have slept for hours, I'm so hungry. Easing herself slowly onto her side, lifting her head cautiously—the headache was gone. She dared to sit then, swing her small feet over the side of the bed. I'm so hungry, it must be suppertime, and poor Walter, he must be starving, too.

She looked at her watch, closed her eyes and slowly

opened them, looked again. It wasn't possible. It must have stopped, or she couldn't read it properly, in this dim light. She closed her eyes and pulled the chain on her bedside lamp, then slowly, cautiously, opened her eyes again. Still no pain shot through. It was safe. But the clock on the table said two-fifteen. Her watch said two-fifteen. Could they both be wrong? The sweep hand on the clock was still sweeping—

Grace Wyndham lay back on the bed again. Her headaches were always capricious, coming and leaving with an abruptness that she despised. But this was the last straw, that her terrible wracking pain would choose to stop right after Walter's prayer.

Ten minutes later, Walter poked his nose into the room and withdrew it quickly, grinning. When his mother had a headache, she lay on her back, her body stiff with tension. Now she relaxed on her side, and a red and white candy wrapper lay on the blanket. She had been up, moving about. Whether she admitted it or not, the Lord had cured her, praise God!

He went downstairs and roamed around the quiet house, thinking about his plans for the future and wondering who could advise him best. His old friends wouldn't do, his Uncle George would say he should ask his mother, do what she thinks best. Kate Thorne? No, she was too establishment by far, her father was more with it than she was. Simon? No—he stopped in the middle of the center hall. What a simpleton he was!

There was only one person who knew all the answers. Brought up to kneel when he wanted to pray, down on his knees with bent head, he took pleasure now in throwing his arms high, here in the center of his mother's house. Head back, face glowing, he called on his Lord.

"Father, in the name of Jesus, I ask Your help."

Walter lowered his arms. At Friday night prayer meeting, Camilla Frey had told about laying a fleece before the Lord. What was it? Yes—she'd wanted to teach the confirmation class again this year, but she didn't want to cause trouble for the new minister. So Camilla put a fleece before the Lord. She told Him to fix it up if He wanted her to teach. He must make it possible, and she would wait until a certain day. The day before her deadline, the very evening before, Mr. Thorne called and asked her to teach the class. Praise God!

"Eleven fifty-nine," someone had said, laughing. "The Lord likes to wait until the last possible moment."

Walter had waited until the last possible moment already. He realized that as he sat on the steps, remembering Camilla's fleece. School began in a week.

He spoke softly. "Lord," he said, "I want to do Your will. If You believe I should go back to the University next weekend, give me a sign, some proof of Your will, something that will take away my uncertainty. Bring it soon, Lord." He thought a moment longer, and added, "Like before next Friday, please!"

On Wednesday, his mother nibbled lettuce and cottage cheese for lunch, attacking the problem of weight head-on. The dressing she put on top of the cottage cheese spoiled the attack, but made the rest palatable. While she nibbled, she looked through the mail and nagged Walter.

"Being casual about clothes is normal, I'm sure," she said, and dropped the letter asking about money for the community concert program onto a pile at her left. "Being absolutely sloppy about them is hardly necessary, Walter, especially for you. No matter what you actually wear, dear—" she paused to look twice at the church calendar for the month, which arrived with the parish letter that morning. There it was, actually on the page—"charismatic prayer and praise meeting, Friday night, eight o'clock, north parlor." Mrs. Wyndham read it twice and looked over her reading glasses at Walter, eating lunch as though he might never be offered food again. He looked so normal!

"As I was saying, no matter what you choose to wear, Walter, there are certain things a gentleman must have in his closet, to be prepared for any eventuality."

"Yes, of course, mother, but we did all that a year ago. Nothing's worn out, you know."

"I have no difficulty believing that. You've worn nothing but that pair of blue jeans as far as I can tell."

"Comfort is the key word," he said cheerfully, holding out his glass for her to fill with milk. All this fussing about clothes, when for all he knew he might never return to campus—it was hard on his appetite. Increased it, actually.

His mother pushed a letter across the table.

"This is for you," she said. He looked at it curiously, while she dribbled a little more dressing on her cottage cheese and finished her salad.

It was postmarked the state capital; the University was in the state capital. He opened the letter carefully.

"My dear Wyndham," the letter began. Walter glanced at the signature, read the rest of the letter quickly. It was from the preacher, the black cat who'd led him to the Lord. Pastor Luke was recommending him to work with small boys in a new "Friendly House" near the campus.

"I don't know whether or not you like to work with youngsters, but this spot requires a Spirit-filled Christian, and I know you are that. I am sure you will bring love and understanding to this job if you can work it into your schedule. They requested a student, and your name came at once to my mind. If you are interested, come and see me as soon as you are back on campus and settled in. Yours in Christ . . ."

Walter read the letter twice. Surely this was the work of the Lord, the answer to his fleece. His mother watched, curiously.

"I suppose—if you really think I need new clothes, mother, I could go shopping this afternoon."

The diversion worked. She leaned back, smiling benevolently. "Of course, and high time, young man. You ought to begin packing, too. The week will be gone before you know it."

He told her not to worry, he would be packed in plenty of time, and he would buy out the stores that very afternoon—which exaggeration took her mind completely away from his letter and any good advice she might have offered, and turned it onto money and spending it wisely, not getting things he wouldn't need. She followed him to the door, anxiously reminding him that his father had not put money in the bank by spending it foolishly.

He backed the sleek car out of the carriage house, turned it around, and stopped at the place where the drive angled around the house. Man, he'd taken a big chunk from the hedge again, last night. Another two feet and he would have clipped the house itself. Ah, well— He made a mental note to himself to fix up those broken branches, clip the hedge when he came back, and to come around more carefully next time. He knew better, but sometimes he felt too great to slow down.

Chapter Seventeen

AT THEIR MEETING on the second Tuesday in October, the official board of the church commended John for inviting the ecumenical prayer and praise group to meet in the parlors, although eight of the ten members could not have explained what the group was all about. Friday was not the night they cared to spend at church, but they agreed that it showed a fine sense of community. They were not, after all, looking for trouble, and the church furnace, which was old, and the paint, which was flaking, were more important at the moment.

The time for making pledges arrived, and Larry Spencer remarked to John that he was certainly surprised, the Christ Church people who went to that damn meeting had all increased their pledges. "At least they put their money where their mouth is," he said, and went on adding figures.

Nora brought the number of cranes to six hundred and

one, with a flurry of paper folding after the first week of school. Now homework and friends kept her happily busy; Margaret suggested one day that they might remove the flying horde. Nora refused, said they reminded her of how lucky she was to be in this great town with all these great kids, and besides, she liked having six hundred and one cranes flying over her head.

Pete complained that the football team didn't win quite enough, and Judy wouldn't date him often enough; except for those two things, he liked Bentley Falls just fine. When he succeeded in talking Judy into watching football with him, instead of attending prayer meeting, he was completely happy. When she refused, he found another date, and what better way to meet people, than to date more girls? Girls, John told him one day, were like streetcars—there'll be another along in a minute. Pete had never seen a streetcar, but he caught his father's point, and borrowed the car to take another streetcar out.

Margaret was contented because her family was. Sometimes on Friday nights she stood by the kitchen window, wondering about the meeting across the way, but she never suggested going. That would be up to John. When—and if—he wanted to attend, she would go along. Meanwhile, the Lord was real enough to her now, and she praised His name in ordinary English gratefully, thanking Him for the joy received and the joy to come.

Kate sometimes thought wistfully of other days and other places. She remembered her small room in Cleveland, and the students she'd struggled to help, and worried about them. This year was totally different, but at least she'd discovered she could teach a larger class, and—usually—enjoy it. Living in the midst of her family, she had few moments alone to remember.

She survived the first PTA meeting, attended most of

the football games, learned the names of all the faculty members and the students in her classes, and found she could digest a sandwich brought from home more easily than the cafeteria food. She saw very little of Alex.

They met at teachers' meetings, of course, and in the office if he happened to be around when she checked her mailbox twice a day. He always called her "Miss Thorne," most respectfully.

His presence in a classroom brought instant silence, and she was grateful that he stopped in her huge study hall several times the first few weeks. Still, no one could possibly suspect they had ever danced together, she thought. His attitude was strictly business; she called him "Mr. Gore," and was sometimes irritated, sometimes amused. Him principal, me teacher, she thought, passing him in the hall. And that's a good thing. He could obviously live without her, and she could certainly manage without him. She instinctively knew when he was around; he always appeared when she needed help. She convinced herself that this was normal.

On the twenty-second, however, late on that Thursday afternoon, Alex came into her room.

"Of course you know it's nearly five o'clock?"

Looking up from reading Tim Bowman's theme, she surprised herself by feeling unexpectedly pleased and thinking how nice he looked, leaning against her door.

"Is it really that late? I'm almost finished."

"You have no business here after the building is empty, Kate. It isn't safe."

"Ridiculous." She put the paper down and looked curiously at him. So she was Kate, again? "In the first place, the building is never empty, quite. And besides—"

"It isn't ridiculous. Take your papers home when it gets this late." He sounded irritated. He crossed the room and stood by the window, looking down at the parking lot. "I've noticed you are usually the last to leave, and I don't like—"

"Come now, Mr. Gore, sir. You may be the principal, but you can't tell me when to go home. I like grading papers here, especially themes. It's quiet—no television, no stereo." She shook the papers into a pile and put them into a folder. "However, I'll go quietly. I didn't realize it was after five."

"Good." He continued to stare into the parking lot while she unlocked the closet and put her coat on, locked the door again. When she picked up her folder, he went to the door.

"I'll walk you to the car," he said. "I have a favor to ask."

She stopped at the outside door and looked at papers and leaves blowing furiously in the October wind, and turned to Alex.

"It's cold out there," she said. "What kind of favor, Alex?"

"I'll explain in the car." He pushed her gently out and turned to check the lock on the heavy door. She ran for the car, holding the folder tight against her, keeping out the wind—it was cold. Inside the car, she watched as he raced down the walk, yanked open the door, and landed on the seat beside her.

"Hello, Kate," he said.

"Miss Thorne, to you."

"Inside, Miss Thorne. Out here, Kate."

"Still school property," she said, and he lifted his shoulders and said he did his best, but no one was perfect.

"We could go somewhere for coffee? Not home, but somewhere close? Nan's at home, you see."

"Frankly, I don't see, but I can't go for coffee now, Alex. It's too late."

"Oh. Well." He looked embarrassed; Kate leaned against the steering wheel and waited. He started this—after two months of formality. This sudden drop into friendship was unexpected and, she wasn't sure, possibly not desirable. But she would decide that after she'd heard him out. Since there was no alternative, this being her car.

"Kate, you remember Labor Day weekend, the night we went to dinner, and the kids on the beach?"

"It isn't something one forgets," she said. "At least, not the kids on the beach. Have you decided to take over the beach ministry?"

"My God, no!" His face clouded with remembered anger, and then relaxed again. "It started that night, though. Nan keeps saying she wants to go to a prayer meeting, see what's really happening. Kate, I've argued myself blue. I can't argue anymore. Just to see, she says."

"She means because of Simon, of course. You know that, Alex. It hasn't anything to do with the kids on the beach. She wants to see what Simon sees, be where he is."

His dark eyebrows went up in surprise. He considered that, and gave a whoop of laughter. "Trust one female to see through another," he said, finally, and laughed again. "Bless the little love, and blast her, too, for getting me into such a funk. Last night she announced she was, by damn, going to the church, and I've been biting heads off all day, thanks to her. You really think it's a ploy?"

Kate studied his face. Could a man be so wrapped up in his work that he never saw the one he lived with? His own sister?

"She loves him, Alex. I know that, and I've seen them together only a few times. You must know it."

"The year Nan spent in bed with rheumatic fever, he came out often, you know. We needed his friendship, and I guess he needed ours. Those were miserable times for him—"

"Simon miserable?" Kate found that hard to accept, and told him so.

"No, really. He and his dad had slightly different—well, actually, totally different concepts of how to run a store, and his father wasn't about to let Simon take over. He felt trapped, because he knew they needed and loved him, yet they wouldn't allow him to *be* him— I'm not making sense."

"Yes, you are. I've wondered about Simon."

"He's a frustrated artist, never felt he had the talent to make it for himself that way, though—"

"But he has the right personality for a salesman, Alex, doesn't he?"

"You bet, and a good one. But he wasn't permitted to put his selling ideas into practice, and he lacked the talent to become an artist and forget the world of merchandising, or the streak of cruelty necessary to leave two aging parents." Alex unbuttoned his coat and leaned back against the seat. "His parents are already past sixty," he said. "So he figured he was trapped, and had just reached the point where he was willing to say to hell with the whole bit, and take off for God knows where, when this religion thing caught hold. You could say, I think, that it saved Simon, but by gosh, Kate, it's not going to get Nan! I don't want her involved in it."

"It isn't the worst thing that could happen to her, Alex."

"Proper answer for a minister's daughter. But doesn't change my opinion."

"Then keep her away from the meeting. Don't forget, Simon said it was like sitting on a riverbank, very easy to slide in."

"She'd better not slide. Look, Kate, what I wanted to ask you—what I still want to ask you—would you go to that meeting with her tomorrow night?"

"No," she said.

He looked startled, and she enjoyed the anger that flared up in her own mind. Didn't he know that she could refuse him, after school hours? Her Friday nights were not his to dispose of, and she would not, under any circumstances, go to another prayer meeting, anyhow.

"I can't go, Kate. We have a home game, and besides, after the hard time I've given Simon, I don't dare show up there."

"I see that. You *can't* go, and I *won't* go." Kate's dimple went in. "Let Nan go alone, Alex. If she slides in, Simon can catch her, and that's not a bad idea."

"It's a rotten idea! I don't want her sliding in—all that emotional stuff, the healings, the tongue-speaking—it's got to be phony. You know that, Kate."

He looked out the window, apparently studying the empty bicycle racks. Kate sat quietly. Finally he turned to her again.

"Listen, Kate, couldn't you go, this once? I don't want Nan involved, but I can't stop her going. I'm only a brother, after all. And she's of age, worse luck. But if you would go along, to keep her steady? Wouldn't you?"

She'd be damned if she would—but she didn't say that. Staring out the windshield, watching small figures in the distance, running and tumbling—football players working out, she supposed—she remembered the two months since their last evening together, the way he'd reduced their relationship to teacher and boss. Why should she do anything for him, much less why should she go the last place in the world she wanted to go? She'd be damned if—

"All right, Alex. Once. But only once, you understand. If Nan goes again, she'll go with Simon or herself."

He slumped in the seat, pulled himself up again quickly. "Thank you, Kate," he said.

"I'll call tonight, say that you mentioned she was going and ask if I can go along."

"She'll suspect me."

"No, I'll be careful. But just this one time."

He reached for her hands and held them lightly in his own. "Kate, it's been murder, you masquerading as Miss Thorne of Room 24. I wish—"

"Don't spoil it, Alex. You asked a favor and I said I'd help, that's all. You've made it abundantly clear that our relationship is teacher and principal, and I like it that way. I'll be glad to see Nan again, however."

He didn't resist when she pulled her hands away, but he made no move to go, either. His next words came slowly.

"In an isolated school such as ours, the relationship I am concerned about in the fall, next to student and teacher, of course, is that of teacher to teacher. I thought it was terribly important that you have a fair start, Kate, without anyone thinking we were other than—"

"Isn't that rather ridiculous?" She interrupted him. "I mean, in the first place we are not 'other than,' whatever that means. In the second place, it's perfectly all right."

"First place, second place—do you help with the sermons?"

"You really have a thing about preacher's daughters, don't you? I knew that the day we met. One bite you once?"

"Never gave one a chance, marked them down early as a type to avoid. Until you came along, Kate. How about Saturday night?"

"No. I said I'd call Nan and that's what I'll do. You needn't put honey on it, Alex. I'm not fond of honey. I'm going to be late for my dinner if you don't get out. See you tomorrow, no doubt." She turned the key and the motor caught. Alex opened the door. He grabbed before the wind blew it away, and held tight as he leaned back in the car, said just wait—just wait, he shouted, and slammed the door. He stood alone in the almost empty lot as she backed the car around and went toward the road. She did not wave. She was furious with herself and with him, disgusted that she'd promised to go with Nan, disgusted that he'd begun to ask for a date and she'd cut him off too soon, she should have let him go on and *then* refused. Why did I promise? Now I'll have to call Nan. She felt herself grow tense, thinking about it. God, I don't want to attend that prayer meeting. It isn't because I don't want to praise You, it's because—because—

Because I'm scared. Not of sliding off the slippery bank, not me. But scared of the things they do, the praying in tongues, just for instance.

Still, I must call Nan. Before eight o'clock. If I wait longer than that, I'll talk myself out of doing it. Just my luck to get a principal who is too sound for his own good—in this isolated school the relationship I am most concerned with is that of teacher to teacher—rot! Rot and double rot. He thinks a preacher's daughter will wallow in religion, that's his trouble. I never wallow. Never, never never! He's a very easy man to hate.

She drove the seven miles home arguing with such rational thought all the way, but she did call Nan. At seven fifty-nine, she went to the phone and was relieved when Nan was delighted.

"Simon said you'd come back some day. He'll be so glad!"

He needn't be, Kate thought, hanging up. She wasn't going out of some deep, emotional need; she was going because Alex asked her to. And that's a pretty idiotic reason, come to think of it. She reached a hand out to call Nan, say she'd changed her mind, but drew it back. A promise is a promise, and I said I'd do it. Just this once.

Washing dishes at the kitchen sink the following night, Kate watched the cars turning into the church lot across the drive, a steady stream of headlights, and people walking toward the back door of the parish house.

"A dance I could understand," she said, scrubbing a pan viciously. "A movie, even a TGIF club, but this is unbelievable!"

"What's TGIF?" Nora stopped drying a plate to figure that out, and Pete, shrugging into his coat on his way through the kitchen, explained.

"Thank God It's Friday, stupid," he said, and Nora said if they knew of a club like that, she'd join. She was glad it was Friday.

"My dumb math teacher," she began. Her siblings groaned in unison and told her to cut it; it was her single but constant complaint about the new school.

"Make a dozen new cranes—maybe he'll break a leg," Pete suggested, and she pretended to consider this, said it would probably take two dozen and she didn't really have the time to fold two dozen cranes—

"Nora, no more cranes!" Margaret came into the kitchen, told Kate that Nan was here, and that she would finish the dishes. "Though why we're so late tonight, I don't know."

"Friday," Kate said, as though that explained everything, and went to greet Nan.

"Shall we cut through the backyard?"

"No, the other way." Nan looked as nervous as Kate felt. "Let's walk around the corner."

Kate buttoned the top button of her coat and hunched her shoulders, but yesterday's wind was gone. It was a silent kind of night, with clouds hiding the stars.

"Are you sure you want to go?"

"Yes, I made up my mind. I mean, I think it's nonsense, but Simon—" Nan's voice trailed away; Kate could finish the sentence and it required no answer. They walked in silence until they passed the steps leading up to the nave door.

"Do they meet in the parlor?"

"I think so."

Inside, they stood uncertainly. People moved around the hall, hugging one another and laughing, greeting each other.

"You'd think they only met once a year, rather than once a week, wouldn't you? Huggingest gang I've ever seen," Kate said, just as she herself was caught from behind and lifted from the floor. "Simon!"

"How about that! You're here! Nan—" He hugged Nan, too, his face glowing as though they were the two people he'd most wanted to see in all this world. He hung their coats and led them into the large front parlor, where chairs were put in a large circle, several rows of chairs, most of them already filled.

"Not the front, Simon, good gosh—the back." Kate protested against being led to the center of the circle, and cut behind the rows of chairs to some empty places.

Simon called her coward, but sat beside Nan, and moments later the singing began. He reached for songsheets from an empty chair and they joined in. Camp songs, Nan whispered, and Kate nodded. They were, many of them, the same songs she'd learned in church camp years ago. But no campfire, she thought, unless—maybe here—the fire was invisible.

A movement behind caught her attention; she turned quickly, in time to see a flowered blouse, a watching face pulled back.

Leah. Oh, my soul, that's Leah. Kate forgot to sing as she considered the possible reasons Leah might have for being in the next room, watching the charismaniacs.

Chapter Eighteen

I saw the Lord,
I saw the Lord,
He was high and lifted up,
And His train filled the temple,
And the angels cried, "Holy,"
The angels cried "Holy,"
The angels cried "Holy is the Lord."

IT WASN'T a hymn, exactly. The words were from Isaiah, and someone in Texas or California had found a tune, taught it to a few people who taught it to others, and now, wherever charismatic groups met, you could hear it. They knew it in Idaho and Ohio, in West Virginia and Florida. The heavyset bald man in the front row of the circle learned it in Chicago and included it in the Bentley Falls song sheets. His secretary typed the words and mimeographed them, and thought it was a funny kind of job—but he was the boss. Curiosity brought her to a meeting, and she and her husband were regulars now.

"It's because they are happy Christians," she would explain, if you asked.

Teenagers filled the second row, halfway around the circle, sang louder than the others, and kept the tempo going when the others began to drag. They testified without embarrassment because they were glad.

"It's beautiful, knowing Jesus," one boy said.

"Fantastic," another said, and the first boy said that's what it was, all right, Jesus was fantastic.

"I was sure the Lord wouldn't want me," he explained. "I was too rotten, too sinful, like Paul said, but He wanted me anyhow. He loves me just the way I am, and now I can do anything I want to do."

He paused, and several adult voices began to speak, protesting, when he laughed joyously and added, "The thing is, I can do anything I want to do, but the Lord has changed the things I want! Praise the Lord!"

Craig Blanshard spoke. "I don't suppose I'll ever understand Revelations," he said. "I wonder, when I read it, whether anyone ever has. But the other day I read this verse again, and I praised God. 'Behold, I stand at the door and knock; if any man hear my voice and open the door, I will come in to him, and will sup with him, and he with me.' There isn't anything in that verse about me getting perfect first. All I have to do is open the door. Praise God!"

The crowd sat silently after he sat down, silent, that is, except for the usual, murmured prayers. Kate thought about his final words and wondered—was it really as simple as that?

Did Jesus come in, just like that?

Would He?

For that matter, *could* He?

Judy Lawson waved a letter over her head, said it was from Walter. "To all of us," she explained. "He sends his love and wants us to know that classes have started—says we should say a prayer for his philosophy professor. He's working two hours every afternoon with some boys in what they call a Friendly House, must be like our Neighborhood House, and would we pray for his boys, please? And he especially wants us to know that he's found five other Spirit-filled Christians in the dorm, and they have prayer together every night, and he knows the group will grow because already other fellows have stopped by to listen, and ask questions. Isn't that fantastic?"

They all agreed it was, and Craig asked if someone would sit in proxy for all the college students. He felt led to pray especially for them, that the Spirit might lead them. One of the boys went forward and sat in the chair pulled to the center of the room. Others gathered around and laid hands on him.

Nan poked Kate gently, and whispered. "That looks like Larry Spencer."

"Isobel's husband?"

Nan nodded, and Kate studied the back of his head. What in the world brought him to a prayer meeting?

Isobel explained that, later on. When they broke for coffee, Kate and Nan decided to leave, and Simon offered to take them out for coffee. As they put on their coats, Isobel rushed up.

"I'm so glad you're here, so glad! Did you see Larry?" She nodded toward her husband, shrugging into a thick black topcoat, and lowered her voice to a shrill whisper. "He came to be sure we weren't hurting his church, that we were orderly. Can you imagine? The new carpeting and all—but he stayed all this time. We're going now, but he stayed all this time!"

As she spoke she darted glances at Kate, as if she had more to say if she dared. Kate shrank away, moved close to Simon. The woman gave her the shivers. Larry came up, holding Isobel's coat, and smiled when she introduced Kate.

"I don't know, Miss Thorne. I'm sure your father meant well, but that's a big crowd for our parlor. I wonder—"

"Now, Larry, it was a nice quiet meeting, you said so yourself. And lovely people, some of our neighbors, even. There isn't a thing to worry about." Isobel's eyes flicked at Kate again; she smiled nervously.

Simon told Larry he should be more ecumenical—that was the popular word in church today. Christ Church was setting a fine example, and he should welcome these outsiders. He laughed, but Larry nodded seriously and said he couldn't quite bring himself to see religion that way.

"I don't like it," he said.

"But he stayed, Simon. He stayed all this time." Isobel's thin voice rose in a gleeful crescendo, as she put her arm through Larry's and with a quick, odd look at Kate, led him out the door.

Kate remembered Leah, and asked the others to wait. She went to the doorway of the small classroom beyond the parlor and opened the door. Leah was perched on the edge of a chair, beside the folding doors that could open into the larger room.

"There are empty seats out there, Leah," Kate said, snapping on the light. "Why peek through the crack? Afraid someone would see you? Or—" she stopped. "Are you all right?"

"Yes, of course I am. You startled me is all. I know it's

wrong to spy, Kate, but Aunt Grace said— It's not for me to say, you know, but how can we know what's happening if someone isn't watching?"

"But Leah, you'd be welcome in the parlor. They are really friendly, loving people, and it is your church, too, for heaven's sake. You could—"

"I couldn't—oh, I couldn't. But they pray as if— Do they really expect those people to be healed?"

"Well, I guess they do." Kate had wondered the same thing herself. "It depends on faith, they say."

"Oh." Leah accepted that, gave a nervous shiver and pulled the brown sweater close, hiding the flowered blouse. "What Aunt Grace will say about Walter, though, having prayer in the dormitory, and he hasn't written to her yet, not a word, you know? Oh, I hate to tell her!"

"Then for heaven's sake don't tell her, Leah. If it would upset her, don't tell her."

"Don't tell her?" Leah shrank further into the brown sweater. "I have to tell her. She'll ask, you know. She'll want to know who was here and everything they said—"

"Oh, for crying out loud!" Kate turned and went into the hall again, closing the door behind her. She found Nan and Simon and was about to wish them good night, when she caught Nan's eye. Obviously, Nan was not ready to discuss the prayer meeting alone with Simon, and also obviously, she was afraid she would have to, if Kate left them.

"Tell you what," she said. "Let's go next door. I make a good cup of coffee, and we can be comfortable."

Nan flashed her thank you with a smile. They walked through the parking lot, and Kate led them in the back door, through the kitchen, into the living room.

Alex was there, waiting for her.

Kate opened her mouth. Nan interrupted before a word came out.

"Come to check up on your little sister? Honestly, Alex Gore, I am surprised. It isn't any of your business, you know, where I—"

"I trust you won't be too disappointed, Nannie, when I tell you I came to see Kate, not to check on you. Greetings, Simon. We won the game tonight, Kate, first time this season, and you had to miss it! See what happens when you take up religion?"

"Alex, really?" For a moment Kate forgot the surprise of his appearance and thought about their boys, the players who tried so often and lost always—no, not always—not tonight. Three of the players, the quarterback and two from the backfield, sat in the back of her second period junior English class. Monday would be a joyous day. They would be so proud. They would not have their work done, but—

"Did they honestly win? Legally?" Nan was doubtful, too.

"Twelve to thirteen. Not," he admitted, "much of a win, but it counts. How was your evening?"

"Exhausting." Nan greeted Mr. and Mrs. Thorne and dropped into the green chair. "Kind of like watching a three-ring circus."

"Hey—" Simon complained that she was unfair and she laughed.

"Yes, but it was a little. They all tend to talk at once sometimes," she said to Mr. Thorne. "And if your congregation would sing as enthusiastically as that crowd, you'd think the world was ending."

"Or just beginning," Simon said. Kate said she would make the coffee, and escaped to the kitchen. Alex followed her, telling about the game, which player made what touchdown and extra point, and the touchdown their opponents almost made during the last minute of play.

"Their man fumbled it. We were that lucky tonight," he said. As Kate plugged in the coffeepot he asked about the prayer meeting.

"Was it awful? Nan didn't—"

"It wasn't too bad, Alex. It's strange, sitting there, but you feel as though God must really be listening, as though He couldn't ignore them, they have such faith. Nan felt that, too."

"Oh, Lord—I suppose she'll want to go again."

Margaret came and said the others wanted to hear about the game. Alex went back.

"I'm dragging your father to bed, Kate. Did you find the cookies? There's cheese, too, and crackers."

"I found the cookies, but the cheese sounds better." Kate opened the refrigerator door. "You don't have to go to bed, mother. We like your company."

"I'm glad of that, but dad has a big day tomorrow. A funeral in the morning and a wedding in the afternoon. I always dislike them coming together like that, but perhaps it is a good thing."

Kate looked at her mother, amused. "As long as the bride doesn't see the funeral flowers."

"Oh, no, they always change the flowers, of course. And the bride doesn't usually know the other service took place. But often the grieving family know, and I think it brings them a little happiness. I really do."

"You're probably right."

Kate dawdled in the kitchen, gathering crackers and cheese, cups and saucers, and waited for the coffee to perk. She wasn't at all eager to join the others. But we can talk about the game, she thought. She heard her parents go upstairs and wished they wouldn't, then stood, disgusted

with herself. What are you afraid of, Kate Thorne? Alex—
Her fingers trembled a little as she poured the coffee; she
told herself it was fear. The men might quarrel. She wished
he had not come.

Smiling a little, because a hostess must, above all, smile,
she carried the tray into the living room.

"Simon, I have a question." Nan paused to take a slice
of cheese and a cracker; Alex groaned.

"About the weather, I hope? Snow any day now."

"Right on your little pointed head, I hope—but my
question isn't about the snow. About the fat woman, you
remember, Kate. The time she spoke out loud—very loud,
in fact—in some awful language, if it was a language, and
after a long silence some man in back answered her. He
talked like a page from the King James Bible— If ever
anything sounded phony—"

"She spoke in tongues, Nan. The man interpreted. I
know it sounded funny, but I'm sure he sincerely felt that
God gave him the words. We can't judge that."

"No, but I don't believe for a minute that God speaks
to twentieth-century Americans in archaic language. Why
should He?"

"For myself, I don't believe it either." Simon broke a
cracker and poised a piece of cheese on it. "The few times
I've felt that I was given an interpretation, and had the
courage to speak up—and that does take courage, Nan—
the words have been as ordinary as these I'm using now. But
for that particular man, if he'd thought in plain English, he
would never have believed it was God, you see? I think the
Lord reaches us in the language we'll accept."

"No doubt." Alex pulled out a pipe and made an
elaborate business of filling it. "Lucky He doesn't try to get
through to me. Lord knows what language He'd have to
use."

~ 177 ~

"Pig latin, most likely," Nan said. "Tell me about the healings, Simon. Do people ever really get healed? Does anything ever happen there, that you can see? And prove?"

"Yes. Absolutely. Time and again, Nan, the week following a particular prayer, the person prayed for has come to give testimony. In one four-day period last spring, Dr. Trent—you know, the orthopedic man—lost three patients. There were three people healed."

"Really?"

"Really. In each case he'd seen them the week before, told them an operation would be needed, or months of special care, and the following week he saw each one and admitted the change—the miracle—had taken place. No one told him the Lord had taken charge, however. They missed a great opportunity to witness."

"Dr. Trent has never been famous for his ability to diagnose," Alex said and Simon shrugged, lifted his red brows, and laughed.

"Alex, old buddy, scoff if you like. It's true."

Nan sat chewing on a cracker, ignoring her brother. Kate fervently wished someone would empty a cup so that she could escape to the kitchen and fill it.

"Miracles do happen, Nan," Simon said. "And Jesus is Lord, and alive today as surely as we're sitting here. Now shall we discuss the football game, before your brother wrecks his pipe, scraping it? I always understood that one should first smoke the pipe, and then scrape it."

They did talk of other things, until Nan insisted they must go home. All four stood by the door a moment, and then Kate was alone. She turned to the living room and the empty cups, and Alex came back.

"Told them I forgot something," he said. "Shouldn't you lock the door?"

"I will—though Pete isn't in, yet. What did you forget?"

"If Pete isn't in, that's a rather substantial ghost in the kitchen, eating tomorrow's lunch."

Kate went to the hall. It was Pete, and he was eating. Naturally. He was usually eating. He came out now, a sandwich in one hand, a glass of milk in the other.

"Don't mind me," he said. "Just passing through." He walked up the stairs, turning at the halfway point to tell them Bentley Falls won tonight, and wasn't that something?

They bragged about their winning team, and he went upstairs.

"Early yet," he told Alex. "No need to leave."

Alex looked at Kate, and she laughed a little self-consciously.

"They think I'm lonely," she said. "Pete worries that I don't go out enough, thinks I'm destined to be an old maid."

"Highly unlikely," Alex said. She was holding a coffee cup in each hand, and he removed them, carefully set them on the round table by the door. "Kate, listen—about tomorrow night. Couldn't we have dinner together?"

"So you can talk me into holding Nan's hand again next Friday? No, Alex. Sorry."

"I don't care if you ever speak to Nan again, I just want you, with me—"

"You're a bit giddy," she interrupted. "because we won the game. A normal reaction."

"Kate, I'm warning you—" He raised a hand, palm open, and then pulled her close. His kiss was too short—too long, too fierce, too gentle— It was more than she'd bargained for, and just what she wanted. When it was over, her head stayed on his shoulder, her eyes closed. "I'll pick you up at six?"

~ 179 ~

"Yes," she said. He kissed her again, and the telephone rang.

Kate caught it before the second ring—who could be calling at this hour? Some awful emergency for dad—but it wasn't. It was for her, and the voice was Isobel's.

"Oh, Kate dear, I just knew you wouldn't be in bed yet, and I had to tell you tonight, I was afraid I would lose it by tomorrow, you know, my own nature would convince me by then it wasn't real, and I'm sure it was."

Kate stared wildly at Alex, laughter sputtering out of her; she was unable to answer properly, but Isobel didn't stop for an answer.

"I have to tell you, I was impressed again and again and I know it was the Lord. I couldn't tell you at the meeting, Larry would have died. You know he would have just died if I'd mentioned such a thing, but I'm impressed to tell you the Lord needs you, Kate."

"Isobel, are you all right?"

At the name, Alex leaned against the door, shaking his head and smiling. Kate made a face at him.

"Of course I'm all right. I am to tell you that the Lord needs you. I was impressed with this deeply as I watched you at prayer meeting tonight. I know the Lord has a special purpose in your being here in Bentley Falls, and you must prepare yourself."

"Prepare myself!"

"Of course. You must read the Word and be ready when He needs you. Good night, Kate."

She hung up. Kate replaced the receiver and stared at it thoughtfully.

"She had a message for me from the Lord. Alex, that woman is out of her skull, she's dotty. She says she received the message while watching me at the meeting. She sat two rows in front of us, she couldn't have been watching me—unless she has eyes in the back of her head. Calling at this hour of the night to say the Lord has plans for me, and I should study the Word. That He needs me."

"She's right, except it isn't the Lord," he said. "Those are the very words I had in mind."

Cuddling down beneath the covers, a few minutes later, Kate turned it over to God. You need me, Alex needs me—I don't suppose those needs have much in common.

Any need the Lord might have was far beyond her comprehension, but a contented smile crossed her face as she sleepily considered what Alex might have in mind.

Long after, when she thought she was asleep but wasn't quite, perhaps, she saw David. No, not David, but his violin, and he was playing. Her eyes opened wide and the instrument disappeared, but the music went on, gay and lilting music. Her heart beat faster, in time with the melody until suddenly he stopped, and then, softly, he played the familiar tune of the Benediction, the notes clear and gentle in the night air. "The Lord bless you and keep you . . ."

Kate turned her face against the pillow, and tears ran slowly across her right cheek, dropped from the end of her nose. She let them fall.

Chapter Nineteen

ALEX CAME the next afternoon, carrying an armful of rust-colored mums for Margaret, the very last of the season, he said. They drove north, toward the lake. When Kate asked where they were going, he said he wasn't sure.

"Are you hungry?"

"Not really."

"Good. I'm not either." His right hand reached for hers, their fingers clasped together. When he turned in at the county park, Kate leaned forward.

"Isn't this where we came, that day in August? Isn't it? I remember those trees, that picnic place."

"Right. We sat on that third table, over there, and you spilled ice cream on your bathing suit."

She laughed; she'd forgotten. "It washed off, in the lake," she said.

He stopped at the end of the empty parking lot, facing the lake. They sat looking through the dusk at the water; the lights of a freighter drifted slowly across the horizon and out of sight.

Kate turned to study Alex, his nose—he has a nice, straight nose, she thought—his long, dark sideburns and the hair cut short in back. She curled her fingers, resisting the temptation to touch him, wishing he would say something, anything—

"Kate?" He turned and caught her eye; he exploded into laughter, taking her in his arms at the same moment. "God Almighty, I'm nearly thirty, practically over the hill, and I don't know how to tell a girl I love her! Kate, I love you."

When she could speak again, when she wasn't thinking wildly *Praise God for kisses, for Alex*—when she could make sense, she told him he couldn't, of course, be in love.

"You've only known me for three months, since the first of August."

"Fourth of August, and I fell in love with you the minute you walked into the school and wrinkled your nose as though you smelled something good baking. Of course, I didn't know it was love until I saw you in that yellow bathing suit, looking good enough to—"

"I noticed you noticed."

"Listen, about that afternoon. Only half of me wanted to take you right there on the beach, you know. The other half was saying, 'This is your girl, Gore. You'd better figure out some way to marry her.' "

"That half didn't show, Alex." She smiled. "I was furious because you'd wakened me." She stopped his question with her finger on his lips, and told him about David. About loving him so long, and learning that life went on, and was lonely.

"So you see, Alex, I didn't know how to act, when I felt myself respond to that look."

He kissed her again and said her virtue was safe now, at any rate, since Volkswagens were not designed for lovers. They talked long after the lake disappeared into the dark.

"You invited me for dinner," Kate said at last. "Do you intend to starve me?"

"My appetite has revived, too," he said. "But no food until you promise to marry me."

"I think I'd like that."

"You think?"

"I know. But Alex, not too soon. We ought to know each other better."

"Listen, for two months now I've been pretending— I had two choices, you know, either act like a proper school principal or a soppy idiot—"

"Soppy?" Kate giggled.

"A sophomore in love. Haven't you ever watched a sophomore in love, Kate? That's the way I felt, so I leaned rather backward in the other direction, I guess. But no more—"

"You did lean, rather," she said. "I thought—"

"You shouldn't think." He stopped to kiss her again, and they found that quickly led to another. "Listen, life is ticking away. We could get married next week."

"How about the end of June, after school is out?"

"Thanksgiving vacation," he countered.

"Oh, Alex, we wouldn't dare. Easter time? We have a week vacation then."

"Christmas," he said. "We have two weeks at Christmas."

"Possibly the week after Christmas," she said, laughing. "Dad is too busy the week before."

"Better yet, Christmas afternoon. No one has anything else to do, after dinner."

"Yes, but—" Kate gave a strangled gurgle of laughter as she remembered something. "Don't forget Isobel's message, last night. Who knows what may happen?"

"I'll take the chance," he said, and turned the key. Shifting into reverse, he backed the little car around and started out of the parking lot before he added, "Been a busy time since August, but up here—" he tapped his forehead— "there's a little place with *Kate* written on it, and whenever I had a chance I'd open it and think about you and wonder if I'd really be that lucky, if after all these years I'd really found the girl."

He stopped the car under the streetlight by the main gate and turned to her. "Kate, there is one thing."

"Alex," she said, "I love you."

They agreed the families shouldn't know yet, not until they were more accustomed to the idea themselves, and more decided about the future. They forgot that families do not always require announcements.

When Alex came down the stairs next morning dressed for church, Nan asked if he'd had a good time, last night, if he and Kate had seen a movie or— One look at his face, even before he answered, and she flew across the room to hug him, tears streaming because she was so glad, so glad—

"If you're glad, stop trying to kill me and don't cry about it!"

"I'm not crying. I'm just so happy for you. She's—oh, Alex, she's exactly what I wanted for you!"

When Kate rushed into the kitchen, still tying her robe, saying she'd help with breakfast, she was sorry it was late, but she'd hurry and wasn't it a beautiful morning, Margaret glanced out at the pouring rain, considered Kate's face and said Alex seemed like a fine young man.

"Oh, yes, he is," Kate pushed her hair back and smiled at the toaster. Margaret hugged Pete, spilled Nora's milk, and rushed into John's arms as he entered the back door.

"I really just came for a cup of coffee," he said, laughing at her, and she said, "John, Kate and Alex—"

"Oh," he said, and looked at Kate, too.

Pete said he supposed this meant Kate's room was up for grabs, and if he could move into it, he could turn his smaller one into a darkroom.

Nora stopped mopping up milk. "I could have told you that yesterday," she said. "The way Alex looked when Kate came down the stairs, he didn't look like any old principal to me. He looked exactly like Pete, when Judy sings a solo. Sick."

Margaret invited Nan and Alex for dinner, and Simon, too, because he was with them. As they walked across the backyard after church, Nan told Simon she had a secret to share.

"If you mean the two behind us, there is no secret," he said. "Half a church between them, and the smell of orange blossoms so strong I thought I'd suffocate."

"Oh, Simon—"

"True, on my honor." He laughed. "Didn't you see Alex not watching Kate? I never saw anyone try harder not to watch someone else. I couldn't keep my mind on the sermon for keeping score, and now I'm having dinner with the preacher. How shall I discuss it with him? Intelligently, that is."

Kate heard the last part, and told Simon not to worry. "Discuss the Browns' game instead," she suggested. "He's very nervous about that."

Simon turned and held his arms wide. "Bless you, my children," he said.

"I didn't tell him," Nan said quickly. "He said you reeked of orange blossoms."

"And that's the truth," Simon said.

They were having coffee when John Thorne pushed his chair back and announced that he must leave, he had a visit to make.

This was not uncommon enough to cause surprise, but when he added that Mrs. Wyndham asked him to call, all smiles disappeared. Even Simon's.

"Is she giving you a hard time, sir, about the prayer group meeting in the church?"

"Not yet," John said. "She didn't specify what she was concerned about today."

"But Leah was there," Kate said. "She reported the whole meeting to Aunt Grace, and now she'll be loaded for—"

"Wait, Kate. For all we know, she may have decided the group has merit." John grinned. "Maybe she wants to thank me, ask if she can join."

"Yes, and maybe it's raining silver dollars outside. I wish to heaven—with all due respect, Simon—that the charismaniacs had chosen another church."

"You forget," John said. "I invited them."

"Yes, and I said you were mad when you did it. Aunt Grace—do you know who she reminds me of? Jane Austen's Mrs. Allen. The one who aroused no other emotion than surprise that any man could like her well enough to marry her."

"Oh, I disagree, Kate. She arouses other emotions, including love and admiration from some people. Look at

Leah. And remember, she is only one member of the church."

"True, but how many others are employed by the Wyndham company? And how many older friends can she influence, and—"

"Kate, don't forget the Holy Spirit has a say in all this." Simon stood up and looked across the table at John. "May I go with you, Mr. Thorne? I might be of help, explaining us."

"Thanks, but no, Simon. First we'll see what she is upset about, if anything, and what we can do." John waved at them all cheerfully and went to get his raincoat, but as he walked the three blocks to the Wyndham home, he prayed all the way. For the first time he wished he could pray in tongues. He didn't know what to pray for. Letting the Spirit pray for him would be helpful. Just open your mouth, Craig Blanshard had said. Open your mouth and let the sounds come out, sounds from the Lord.

But I would always wonder, he thought, turning in at the high hedge surrounding Grace Wyndham's home, I would always wonder if those sounds didn't really come from me. He sighed and thrust his hands deeper into his pockets as he went up the long drive, toward trouble.

"Mr. Thorne, did you walk in all this rain?" Grace was the smiling lady of the manor. "Come in, come in and take off that wet coat."

"A refreshing rain," he said. "I enjoyed it." And for a time they discussed the weather, how the rain let up this morning, as people left the church, and began again this afternoon. How it would surely be snowing in a week or so. Or a month or so. Finally John turned the conversation around. Not that he was anxious to get her started, but there was that football game later on that afternoon and also, he knew from experience now, talking was good for her.

"Was there some particular problem, Mrs. Wyndham? Something special on your mind?" That was opening enough, surely. She looked startled, and he suspected she had devised her own offense and now he'd spoiled it. So be it, he thought.

"Problem, Mr. Thorne?" Her cheeks flushed pink, and for a hopeful second he thought she might say no, of course not, and he could go home. But it was a foolish, futile hope. "Indeed, we have a problem," she said, "but I believe we can solve it together. Today. Leah attended the meeting— that meeting—at the church on Friday night, at my request." She paused as though daring him to reprimand her. When he waited silently, she went on.

"I know that your daughter was there, and assume she has given you an accurate picture of the situation. Therefore we can be plain in our speech. According to Leah, only sixteen of the people there were from Christ Church. Now it seems to me, since our other churches were represented, that one of these might provide a meeting place for them. If you would see to that, I will have nothing more to say. It is not my business, I am sure, to worry about where my fellow church members spend their Friday nights."

After this speech, delivered in a rather magnificent fashion, complete with heaving bosom, Grace sat back.

John relaxed in an overstuffed chair, his eyes fixed on the small fire in the grate, and debated his answer. Interesting that she claimed not to worry about where her fellow parishioners spent Friday nights; she'd certainly fussed enough before, when they were meeting in homes.

"You don't think Christ Church is the proper place for prayer and praise?"

"Don't attempt to trap me, Mr. Thorne." She pulled

her shoulders high. "Those meetings are not simply prayer and praise. They are more than that!"

"They are exactly that, Mrs. Wyndham. People gathered together to worship in an atmosphere of love. And on Friday nights our parlors are otherwise empty. I personally feel that fifty people, coming to pray—"

"Perhaps you do, but I do not agree. We have always had the ignorant, the uninhibited, the emotional people in this world, but *not at Christ Church!* We cannot—"

It was his turn to interrupt. "Are you including such people as Craig Blanshard, Wesley Hook, and Camilla Frey? Surely not."

"Perhaps they cannot be called ignorant, but their lack of discipline is appalling. Discipline is the backbone of our nation, and yet these supposedly educated people display their emotions as though they had never known any better. It is not decent behavior."

He could not resist a smile which she noticed immediately despite his quick effort to hide it.

"I see you think it is funny, Mr. Thorne. Is nothing sacred to you?"

"Oh, indeed, yes—"

"It's quite bad enough that Walter—but with him, of course, it is merely a stage. Perhaps we might smile a little, at Walter. I've lived through many of his stages, and I suppose I'll live through many more. But that Christ Church should make room for a bunch of tongue-speaking rabble, I would never have believed. Your responsibility—"

"Not rabble, Mrs. Wyndham." He spoke softly and she ignored him, went on with her speech in a firm voice, the wobbling of her chins the only sign of emotion uncontrolled.

"—is to see that this is stopped. I remember your sermon. You said that the group will fail because of its own foolishness. I remember. But I do not care for Christ Church to become a laughingstock meanwhile." She took a deep breath and added, "I will not have that happen."

"I also said that we would not wish to oppose God, if it turned out to be of His plan." John dared a slight smile.

"It could not be. I am not opposing God, I am opposing Satan. Fake healings and ridiculous gibberings are certainly from Satan." Her voice rose, and John leaned forward.

"Mrs. Wyndham, two thousand years ago Jesus healed people, through the power of the Holy Spirit which was in Him. Jesus is the same yesterday, today and forever—surely you believe that? Why shouldn't He heal today, or last night? Or Friday night, for that matter." He regarded her earnestly. "Have you ever allowed Walter to pray for your headaches? Have you given the Lord a chance to cure you? Have you?"

He watched the blood rise in her neck, become splotches around her eyes. Her mouth made a tight small line across her face; she stared at the fire. John sighed and sat back again. "Are you sure they are led by Satan?" he asked. "For myself, I am not sure of that."

She twisted a lace square between her fingers, reached up and rubbed her forehead with it and then rolled it into a tight ball, all the while looking at the fire, her lips trembling slightly. Finally she heaved herself around and looked directly at him.

"I tried," she said. "You must remember that I tried to discuss this problem with you in a rational manner. I realize, now, that you have no intention of dealing with it, and I shall act in my own way. Of course, I should have known, a minister who allows his daughter to dabble in witchcraft is hardly a person who will—"

John leaped to his feet. "Allows his daughter to what?"

"I'm sure you understand me, Mr. Thorne. Do sit down.

I want you to know that my new grandchild will not be baptized in Christ Church next Sunday. You may remove that from the schedule. It shall not occur. I will notify Alice tonight that she must put off the christening until this nonsense is finished—and it will be finished, you understand."

"Perhaps Alice would rather have the baby christened in her own church, in Toledo?" He controlled his voice carefully. What was that woman talking about, witchcraft?

"Christ Church is still her church. Each of my grandchildren has been baptized here, despite where they may choose to live."

John thought wildly that most babies didn't have a choice about where to live and then pulled his thoughts back in order. He must make her explain her statement . . .

"I'm sorry you feel that way, but about my daughter, you have not yet explained that," he said.

"I wish I could believe you were sorry." She ignored his plea. "Perhaps you will be, however. As of this moment, I shall consider my pledge to the church canceled. I shall not support a church which permits such behavior, which condones practices which are not only irrational but evil." When he did not answer at once, she smiled grimly. "I shall, however, continue to attend. Christ Church was my church long before it was yours; I will be attending it long after you are gone. But while these tongue-speakers meet in my church, I refuse to give my financial support. Is that perfectly clear?"

"Perfectly. I'm happy that you will continue to come. That is most important, after all."

"Is it? I wonder if the Board will agree with you?" Her round eyes looked at him calmly; the chins quivered slightly. Her fingers continued to twist the lace handker-chief. "There is one more thing. Camilla Frey has been teaching the membership classes for years, and has been a sweet and willing helper but surely you must realize she isn't the right person to do that now? She isn't fit to teach the children, Mr. Thorne, and for your own sake, she must be replaced!"

"I fail to see how Mrs. Frey could be anything but good for the young people's class," John said, holding himself carefully, willing himself not to explode. "She has a great deal of empathy with the kids, and this is important. If the Holy Spirit is working through her, how could we do better? Even if it were possible and I could get somebody else," he added.

"It will be possible. As soon as I let it be known through the women's meeting that Camilla is no longer fit for the responsibility."

Good night! John could not sit still any longer. He paced back and forth before the fireplace, trying to choose words that Grace would hear.

"Do you seriously believe—can you imagine—" Obviously she did and she could. Nothing happened at the meeting Friday that should cause this fury in her—unless the news about Walter, the fact that he had not yet written to his mother—was she taking her anger at Walter out on the whole church?

"Do you seriously believe, Mrs. Wyndham, that the church will fail if you remove your support?"

"Others will follow me," she said.

"And do you truly think I can ask a fine woman like Mrs. Frey to step down from a job she does well, with great love, because she prays to God—in whatever language she uses? Our country is built on religious freedom, as well as the discipline you spoke of before, and if some of our people find worshiping God in tongues meaningful, have I any right to stop them? I do not, and neither do you!"

She opened her mouth and he hastily added, "They must be allowed that freedom."

"Not in my church," she said.

John walked toward the door, helped himself to his raincoat from the closet, and slipped into it. Then he turned to Grace Wyndham. She sat like stone in her chair, her fingers twisting the lace the only movement.

"It is not your church," he said slowly. "Nor is it my church. The church is the Body of Christ, the people who believe in Him and worship Him as Lord." She inclined her head slightly and he paused, but she refused to speak.

"The gray stones, the Gothic structure is merely a place to gather, for corporate worship, to keep the rain from our heads, Mrs. Wyndham. If you tore it down tomorrow, the Body of Christ would find another place to gather, I am sure of that. I won't judge this group of worshipers. I do not have the right to judge them. You do not have that right either!"

At this her round eyes opened wider, but she did not speak.

"Christ Church has opened its doors to the charismatic group, and unless the Board decides against them, this will continue. I am sorry as I can be that you find them upsetting, and I will be glad to help you understand them, as I learn to understand them myself."

"Mr. Thorne." She roused herself and stood up. He realized she hadn't heard one word of his excellent speech. Her eyes were glazed. "Before you leave," she said, "there is one more thing. The Bishop will stay with me the night before confirmation Sunday, as is his custom. Normally I invite the Board members and their wives for dinner that night—and the minister too, of course—but this year I shall not do so. There are many things I wish to speak to him about, myself."

John wished her a good afternoon in as gentle a tone as he could command and walked down the steps quickly. Let her believe that last sentence sent fear racing through me, he thought. Let her believe it, it will be good for her. Actually, his main emotion now was sympathy for the Bishop—an evening alone with Grace? God help him!

The important question raised by the last hour was whether Grace spoke for herself alone, or whether she spoke for many of the other members of the church. As he hurried down the street, he knew it was important to discover that, and soon.

But why have a church building if it doesn't serve the needs of the people? John stopped and stared up at the bell tower, at the handsome church door, the newer parish house. Enter, Rest and Pray, the old sign said. This building is dedicated to God. The charismatics are dedicated to God.

He looked back toward Wyndhams. With the leaves nearly gone, he could see the high hedge from here, and the tall elm that stood in the front yard towering over the old house. He wished he could feel satisfaction from his certain knowledge that the tree was sick and would have to be cut down, but the remembrance made him sad. He was fond of elm trees. He was fond of all growing things, including charismatic prayer groups who prayed in ways he dared not pray, who believed with a faith they were willing to proclaim to the whole world.

Willing? Oh, Lord. John walked around to the parish house door. They were more than willing—they were eager to share the good news of Jesus Christ.

He stood inside the quiet hall. The parlor on his right

was the scene of Friday night's prayers. The classroom further down, that must be where Leah sat, watching—spying. Playing 007 for Aunt Grace. And upstairs we worshiped together this morning, he thought. The church was almost filled.

"Oh, be joyful in the Lord, all ye lands—"

Joyful. If it's wrong to praise God with joy, he thought, I'm in the wrong business altogether.

"Lord God, forgive me for losing my temper this afternoon, for not reaching Grace. Help me, with the power of Your Holy Spirit, to keep this church in love. So work through me that all our people will sing for joy."

John grinned at the empty hall, hoped Martin wasn't wandering about to hear him praying out loud on a Sunday afternoon.

Chapter Twenty

THE MONTH OF NOVEMBER closed down the football season. Ford Road School finished next to last in their division, only because the consolidated school across the county line lost every game. Bentley Falls finished third, and the consensus was that next year they would certainly be first. Kate went to the last games, carefully not being with Alex until each one was over, the better to fool faculty and students. It didn't work. By the end of the month, several faculty members were watching them, with interest.

Nan went with Simon to the prayer meetings. She said she needed a good laugh by Friday nights, after teaching first graders all week, and church was a perfect place to get one.

The business of Christ Church moved along despite the outraged feelings of the chairman of the stewardship committee, who announced that three of the oldest members had canceled pledges for the next year—Grace and George Wyndham, and Helen Bentley. John, reporting this to Kate and Margaret as they drank hot chocolate late one night, grinned and said opinions were divided.

"One man said he hoped they'd remove themselves as well as their cash."

"I like that fellow," Kate said.

"He was half-kidding, I think. He did add that Grace had run things for so long, it would be a good chance to see if anyone else knew anything. Craig Blanshard spoke up then, said he was sure the Holy Spirit would solve it if we would be patient and wait."

"Do the men laugh, when he talks like that?" Margaret looked worried as she pushed the plate of cookies toward John.

"They never laugh at Craig—at least, not to his face, not in my presence. They seem to feel that any man who has achieved as much as he has—he's very good in his field, you know, rather well known—and Ivy League, here in the provinces, that counts. If I had a degree from Harvard, Grace Wyndham would consider me a much wiser man." He paused to smile at the thought. "No, the men apparently feel Craig is entitled to talk that way if he likes. They may smile when he brings the Lord into a discussion of the air conditioner, but the feeling is that after all, he's a decent fellow and he just might be right."

"Even Larry Spencer? Isn't he on the Board?" Kate asked.

"He is now—did you know he's still going to the prayer meetings? Comes to protect the church, he says, just in case—"

"That's silly." Margaret laughed. "He knows they won't harm his precious carpeting."

"Of course he does, but he has to have a reason, and

that's the one he started with. I think he also wants to protect Isobel, from what I couldn't say."

"The original male chauvinist, that's Larry." Kate pushed her chair back. "Remember Isobel and her seasickness, how she dreaded sailing? Poor thing!"

"But she got over that. Isobel told me herself she's looking forward to next summer."

"Did she say that?" One up for Simon, Kate thought. "Still, I don't see Larry Spencer speaking in tongues."

"I wonder." Margaret spoke softly, her eyes on the pink china pot. "Happiness like theirs is catching," she said.

"Oh? When are you stepping up to get the Baptism?"

"Me? Oh, Kate—"

"When we accepted Christ as Lord, we received salvation, Kate." John spoke slowly, as though he wanted to make himself very clear. "And when we received salvation by faith, we also received the Holy Spirit, the Comforter. Saint Paul says clearly that not all speak in tongues. Tongues are not the only proof of the indwelling of the Spirit."

"Of course they aren't," Margaret said.

"If they were," John went on, "think of the millions of good Christians for the last several centuries who were not 'in the Spirit.' That's as foolish as saying the light is not on in this room, because from where you are sitting, you cannot see the bulb!"

"Then you've decided tongues are the result of an emotional binge, daddy?"

"I didn't say that. I haven't decided anything of the kind. Having a personal Pentecost is a glorious reality, Kate, as are all of the gifts of the Spirit. But not the *only* reality. These charismaniacs, as you call them, have thrown intellectual argument to the winds and received Christ into themselves, and God bless them, everyone."

He stood up and walked out of the kitchen, went up the stairs toward bed. Kate looked at Margaret.

"My goodness," she said.

"He's been getting phone calls, you know." Margaret smiled. "He's practicing on us."

On the Friday night after Thanksgiving, Kate went to the prayer meeting again. Nan asked her to go, because Simon was meeting with a small group in a nearby town, a group just getting started, who needed guidance. Nan did not want to go alone.

"Absolutely not," Kate said. "Let's go to a movie instead. Alex has to be at school that night."

But on Wednesday, the day before school let out for the welcome, if short, vacation, one of Kate's students came hesitantly to the desk after second period.

"Miss Thorne?" she blushed a bright red, her eyes looked longingly at the door, then back at Kate. "I—oh, I wish I could die!"

"Not right here, please." Kate smiled reassuringly. Nothing could be that bad. "Why do that anyhow, with vacation beginning today?"

The girl giggled and said it was because of her mother. Reaching into the pocket of the daisy-printed smock she wore over jeans, she pulled out a folded paper.

"My mother gave this to me on Monday, said I must give it to you. Please don't laugh, Miss Thorne, she said I must!"

"But I don't know your mother, do I?" Kate tried to remember. "Where do you live?"

"On Ford Road, way south. You don't know her, but she saw you at PTA, and she says she saw you again on Sunday, and the Lord sends you this message."

"Oh, really, Carol."

"I know, Miss Thorne. I know it's dumb, but my mother is a good person, really she is. She insisted I give this to you. She made me promise."

Kate glanced at the note as Carol raced for the door. "Carol!"

The girl stopped and looked back, anxiously.

"Does your mother—does she come to Bentley Falls on Friday nights?"

"Bentley Falls? Goodness no, she goes to our church on Friday nights." Carol giggled. "Not to mention Wednesday and Sunday nights. Honestly, Mother hardly ever goes to Bentley Falls. We live so far out, and the stores are closer in—"

"All right, I just wondered. You'd better hurry to class, Carol."

Long hair flying, the girl obeyed. Kate looked at the note—or not a note, exactly. A Bible reference. Hebrews 4:16.

After school, when Alex poked his head in the door and asked if she wasn't ever coming, she requested a Bible.

"Wash your mouth out, girl. Haven't you heard of the Supreme Court?"

"I know, but wouldn't the library have one? I haven't had time to ask."

He agreed that it should, and they went down the hall. Alex produced the proper key. They went in and found the Bible, in three translations. Kate chose the King James, looked for the reference. She read it slowly and then, eyes wide, read it to Alex.

" 'Let us therefore come boldly unto the throne of grace, that we may obtain mercy, and find grace to help in time of need.' Alex, that's weird. To help in time of need—remember Isobel? I'd forgotten about it, and now look. This, from someone I never even met."

"Rather a wild coincidence, darling, but it is nice to know you're needed."

"If I come boldly to the throne of grace, whatever that means!"

"Before you do that, come boldly with me, I want to—"

"Maybe you do, but first you go to the store with me. Nan and I can't cook a steak dinner for you gentlemen tonight until—" she kissed him quickly—"until you buy the steak!"

But the fun of shopping with Alex and cooking with Nan did not stop her wondering about the note. Finally, as she poured coffee all around the second time, she told Nan she'd changed her mind. She would go to the prayer meeting, after all.

"Over my dead body," Alex said, adding quickly, "Sorry, Simon. But that's no place for my girl. Isn't it enough that my sister is hooked into going?"

"But the Spirit is a gentleman," Simon said, his eyes twinkling. "He won't push himself onto anyone who doesn't ask. You needn't worry."

"And I want to go. I want to see if this girl's mother turns up, Alex. It's all too pat. Two messages from two different places, both purporting to be from your Lord, Simon."

"My Lord? I'll share, Kate."

"You know what I mean. You say you don't know any Mrs. Weatherhead, with a daughter Carol, but I wonder— You couldn't possibly know all those people by name."

He agreed he couldn't, and Alex, reluctantly, gave his blessing on her going. They agreed to meet at Kate's afterward.

"Then, if you slide into Simon's river, I can rescue you," Alex said. "With mouth to mouth resuscitation if necessary."

They were late for the meeting. Slipping in the door, they saw Walter standing in the middle and talking. Kate thought he looked more grown up, as though the two months at school had aged him. He told about the prayer meetings in the dorm, how as many as fifteen to twenty boys joined them each night, and some had received the Baptism through the laying on of hands. "Our hands," he said, with awe in his voice. He told about the children he worked with in the afternoons. "Praise God for this vacation, so that I could come and tell you all about it," he said at last, the boyishness returning to his face as he joined in the laughter and sat down.

They prayed and they sang. Kate was amused because Nan knew most of the songs by heart, now, and almost raised her arms during some of them.

"It feels right," Nan confessed, whispering. "Somehow, you raise your arms and you feel goodness coming into you."

"And the root word of goodness is God," Kate whispered back. "And no doubt—"

"Oh, Kate—" Nan giggled.

When they broke for coffee, Kate went searching for Chris and Craig Blanshard, found them talking to Camilla Frey. Surely these three would know if a Mrs. Weatherhead from South Ford Road ever came to these meetings, or knew Isobel. They said not, and when Isobel herself walked by, Craig pulled her into the group and asked her.

"A Mrs. Weatherhead? My goodness, no, but I know a Mrs. Weatherby. You remember her, Camilla. She came to Christ Church a few times and decided we had too much ritual, you know? She went to the Lutheran Church after that. My goodness, they have more ritual than we have, don't they? But then, I don't believe she stayed there, either. I never did know any Weatherheads, no, I never did."

She hurried away, taking coffee to Larry. "He won't leave his chair," she told them. "I don't see why he won't leave his chair, but praise God he comes."

Craig excused himself, then. "Some people over there need prayer," he said. Chris looked after him, smiling.

"Remember Craig before, Camilla? He hated to speak out loud. He could hardly give a financial report to the Board. He said he was a research chemist so he wouldn't have to talk! Now it's talk all the time, to anyone anywhere—but especially here."

"Well, you know what they say." Mrs. Frey's rosy cheeks grew rosier. "The Holy Spirit makes ordinary people into extraordinary ones."

Kate excused herself to look for Nan. As she moved around a group of people, she came close to the sliding doors of the classroom, and noticed a small crack. Impulsively, she pulled the handle and stared into Leah's eyes.

"Are you still spying for Aunt Grace?"

"Oh, my no, Kate. Please, you won't tell her I come, will you? She thinks I'm watching television at home. Aunt Grace says—"

"But that's ridiculous. She can't have the right to keep you away from here if you want to come."

"But she wouldn't like it." Leah shivered beneath her blue sweater. "I only come because—they're different, and I don't know—they make me feel better. But don't tell Aunt Grace."

"Of course not, why ever should I? But Walter is here. You ought to come out. If this turns you on, enjoy it!" Kate waved an arm toward the people, and Leah drew back into the dark.

"I'd rather not. I'd just rather not."

Kate turned away. Everyone to their own taste, she thought, and if Leah's idea of a fun evening is to hide in a classroom and peek through a crack in a door, who am I to fuss at her? She sighed, and seeing Nan, went up beside her.

"Deliver me from certain foolish people in this world," she began, and realized Nan wasn't listening. She was staring at the group in the corner, three people on chairs, waiting expectantly, and others standing around. Craig Blanshard was talking.

"Don't be afraid," he said, his voice gentle. "If you think you won't receive, that you won't speak in tongues, you are wrong. Everyone who asks, receives."

There was a murmur of assent from the others, mostly men, Kate noted, who stood around the chairs. The three sitting looked pale but excited.

"Of course," Craig went on, "you may be afraid you *will* speak in tongues." A ruffle of sympathetic laughter greeted this. "That's normal, many of us felt that way. We figured we'd take the Spirit, thanks, but not the foolishness that went along with it. But the Lord gives us this sign, this new language; it's part of the package." He moved forward. "We'll just lay hands on you," he said, "and we'll pray with you, but remember, you have to do the talking. Let the Spirit—"

Kate pulled Nan toward the door, gently. "Listen, you'll be slipping in that river, first thing," she said.

Nan smiled at her, without speaking. They put their coats on and Kate led the way down the hall to the back door. "Shorter this way," she said, and Nan nodded.

"You know, all this is very well, Nan, but miracles went out with the first century, you do know that, don't you? And the tongues are a lot of foolish gibberish, anyone can make a noise like an idiot." Kate wasn't sure she believed her own words, but she had to say them, for Alex.

Nan made a face, and laughed, but it wasn't until they reached the house, stood in the hall taking off their coats, that she spoke.

"Remember how I felt before, Kate? As though I wasn't good enough? As if those people had the key to God's inner room and I'd never know what they know? They aren't like that at all. They aren't snobs, or proud, and they have made me see one thing—they've made it clear to me that I do believe. I know Jesus is Lord, Kate. Maybe because they aren't afraid, I'm not afraid either—I believe. I really do." She turned to look at Kate, her face lovely in the lamplight. "Does that make sense?"

"It does, praise God," said a deep voice from the living room. Simon reached long arms for Nan, and as she went into them, Kate went out.

John came into the kitchen from the other door, having escaped from the living room in the nick of time, he told Kate, and added that he wasn't surprised. As he got out his nightly milk and cookies, and offered one to Kate, the back door opened after the smallest of knocks, and Alex came in.

"I started in the front," he said, "but I saw Simon and Nan through the window, and it was obvious they'd never hear my knocking. Has that been going on long?"

"Only a few minutes, and my guess is that you haven't lost a sister, you've gained a brother-in-law. If I call Angelinos, will you go and get a pizza? They're bound to be starving soon."

"I remember, that sort of thing does arouse the appetites. Be right back—stay up, Mr. Thorne, I'll bring a pepperoni one for you."

"And give me indigestion," John said, but he made no move to leave as Alex shut the door softly after himself. Kate called in the order for pizza, thankful the phone was in the hall and out of sight although, she thought, neither Simon nor Nan would have noticed her. She sat at the kitchen table with John, talking quietly, telling about the prayer meeting. She reached her encounter with Leah when he raised his hand, stopping her.

"Listen," he said.

The whispering in the living room had ceased. Simon's voice came clearly to the kitchen.

"Nan, you don't have to go up before all the people at church, you can receive the Baptism in your own room. Anywhere, darling. I know a girl who was driving when she began to pray in tongues. Got so excited she nearly hit a telephone pole— You can receive anywhere, Nan. Right here, if you like. Right now."

"But Simon—" Nan's voice was soft, they could not make out her words, but Simon laughed.

"You can kneel or sit in a chair or stand on your head, I suppose—or stay right here in my arms. Just praise Him, and ask Him in."

Kate clutched John's hand; they stepped softly through the dining room. Nan sat in the green chair, Simon knelt beside her, one big hand covering her shoulder, the other holding her hands. He was praising God with such a look of happiness on his face that Kate looked away; she pushed back against her father.

"Look up, Nan. You mustn't keep your mouth shut, you know—remember Craig telling about Peter, how he had to step out of the boat himself? He had to do the walking across the water. You have to do the speaking. Say the words, any words, any sounds that want to come out. Let them come—but you do the talking. Open your mouth, Nan."

The two in the doorway watched, transfixed. They

listened, and inside Kate prayed for Nan, and knew her father was praying, too. Minutes ticked away on the clock above Kate's head, and still they watched.

Finally, after Nan raised her head, after she said "Thank You, Jesus, praise Your name," her voice broke. "Simon, I can't! It isn't for me, after all. I can't—"

"Nan, what do you hear, inside? Aren't there sounds that want to be spoken?"

"Odd dumb sounds, Simon. Silly sounds. They couldn't be—"

"Say them. Just say them to me, Nan."

"Ohwa laka—that's silly, Simon!"

"It isn't silly, His Spirit is giving you those strange sounds, it's His way of giving you a tongue, Nan. Say them again, and go on."

She repeated the sounds and then said them again, and again, and the next time she went on speaking new sounds, new syllables—a lovely tongue, Kate thought. A beautiful tongue. Nan looked wide-eyed at Simon, and then went on praying, smiling because tears were running down across his freckles. John turned away, taking Kate's hand and drawing her with him to the kitchen.

"Praise God," he whispered.

Kate said, "Yes."

But Alex swore.

He came in with the hot pizza boxes, and Kate caught him, hugged him and said he'd best be quiet, they were praying.

"Nan? That'll be the day."

"Well, listen." She drew him to the doorway into the dining room, stopped and shrugged her shoulders, smiling. "They were praying," she said. "Nan's singing, now."

"Singing?" They listened, and Alex turned to stare at

Kate. "You call that singing? It's gibberish, it's—oh, my God!"

"Alex, it was beautiful, let me tell you about it. Dad and I—"

"I don't want to hear about it," he interrupted, and turned back to the kitchen. John escaped to the hall, where he studied the wallpaper quietly. "Simon got to her—I suspect they deserve each other. Kate, I don't feel like pizza after all, if you don't mind. I'm afraid I'd be unpleasant company."

"Alex, you wouldn't!" She flew to the door and stood with her back to it.

"The hell I wouldn't. She'll come out here looking like the Queen of the May, and I'll—just let me out, honey. I'll see you tomorrow."

"But Nan is your sister!"

"Damn right she is, and I have to live with her. Can you imagine living with someone hung up on religion—oh, good Lord, I'm sorry." He sent an apologetic look at John's back.

"The tolerant Mr. Gore. The first day we met you said there was room for everyone in the church, remember?"

"There is room, but I don't have to like it, Kate. I didn't like the change in Simon, and I doubt I'll care for the new Nancy. Now if you'll move it, sweetheart, and let me out, tell Nan I'm ailing—a headache will do—and I'll go home and go to bed. Maybe by morning I can look her in the eye and say it's great."

"It is great. You mustn't leave, Alex. You can tell her that right now."

"Not with a straight face, I can't. Look, Kate, if you think this is so wonderful, if you're thinking of joining that crowd, let me tell you something. I will never make an ass of myself that way. Never. So don't expect it." He threw his

~ 209 ~

coat on the chair and sat down. Kate came slowly from the door and sat across the table, reached to hold his hands in hers.

"You know it isn't an experience I want," she said. "I couldn't do it either. But that doesn't make it wrong for them."

John came back into the kitchen and Alex grinned at him, not cheerfully. "Still going to let me marry your daughter?"

"Question is, do you want to, when she's so bossy? Better think about that." John sniffed the fragrance from the pizza boxes and sat down. "Your reaction is normal, in my experience, but don't judge yet, Alex."

"I'll try not, but don't forget, I've put up with my buddy in there for a year now, and frankly—"

"Remember Gamaliel," John said, and Kate snorted.

"Ten to one he's never heard of your friend Gamaliel," she said. "But you were there, daddy. Was that of man? Or of God?"

John's answer was lost as Nan danced suddenly into the room, Simon behind her. She pulled Alex to his feet and hugged him, laughing. He threw his arms high in the air in a gesture of despair before returning the hug—and over her head, he spoke to John and Kate.

"See what I mean? The Queen of the May," he said.

Chapter Twenty-One

THE SUNDAY after Thanksgiving was Advent Sunday; John preached about love. Romans 13:8. "Owe no man any thing, but to love one another: for he that loveth another hath fulfilled the law."

At the sermon time, he looked over the congregation and noted the number of students there, including Walter beside Grace, in her usual pew, praise the Lord. He chose this text because of the young people who would be at home for this celebrating weekend, and late Friday night, listening to Alex and Kate, he'd been especially glad of his choice. Now he wondered if perhaps Grace had been the motivation after all; perhaps he was speaking for her, more than all the others.

Not that it mattered; she didn't listen. She frowned at her feet while he spoke. But John also saw Walter, whose eager face took in each word, and from Walter he looked at other young faces, and praised God for them as he talked.

"The night is far gone, the day is at hand—" Did Grace lift her eyes at those words, or did he imagine it? As she went out the door after the service, she did not reach out her hand, but said good morning in icy tones. I shall preach forgiveness next, he thought, for weeks in a row if necessary. George Wyndham smiled, however, his head of white hair bent briefly, and Leah, coming after her father, clasped his hands as though making up for her aunt's manner. Walter grinned and said that was a sermon worth coming home for.

And that would have made John's day, if that afternoon he had not asked the confirmation class about his sermon. Seven blank faces looked at him.

John choked back the laughter rising in his throat—serves me right, he thought. As he searched for words to rescue himself gracefully, Camilla spoke.

"Mr. Thorne preached about love this morning, remember? The same kind of love we've been talking about in class."

"We've been talking about Jesus." A freckle-faced boy looked puzzled, and a blond girl, whose blue jeans and sweater did nothing to hide the fact that she was, indeed, growing up, answered him.

"Of course, dumdum," she said. "About Jesus loving us. Don't you remember anything?"

"Yes, and about how we can love Jesus." Camilla's bright eyes smiled at them all. "Jesus taught that there were two important commandments. Can you recall what they are?"

"I remember, all right, we got to love God and love one another," the freckle-faced boy said. "But—"

"And if we do, we don't have to memorize those ten commandments," another offered, grinning in pleased surprise at himself.

"I'd never remember them anyhow," the freckled one admitted, laughing.

"Listen—" Light dawned suddenly for Tommy, a small dark-haired boy in the circle. "Like Mr. Thorne said this morning—I do remember, sir—if we love one another, and I guess 'one another' includes God, doesn't it? Well, if we do really love one another, we can't break those commandments. Right?" He waited a moment for John's nod. "It's because we don't go around hurting people we love, and if we broke any of those old laws, we'd be doing that, see?"

"Well, of course." The blond girl was confident now. "It's like when I wanted to smoke a cigarette. Well—" she paused to look defiantly at the startled adult faces. "People do smoke in the eighth grade, you know. But I didn't do it, because I could hear my mother—I just knew she'd hate it, and I didn't want to make her unhappy. I tried to think she'd not ever know, but—oh, well, you know. I didn't, anyhow." She tossed blond hair back, over her shoulders.

"That's it, exactly," Camilla beamed at them, her cheeks pink. With a happy look at John, she passed out the prayer books. John sat back and listened.

She spoke of Jesus as a friend, as someone real and alive, who loved them all. This class of young people would be well prepared for reaffirming their baptismal vows.

They were, in fact, reading the service of Baptism now. Camilla led them as they read the questions asked, the answers made for them by their parents, their godparents, and the church. She told them that now they had a chance to agree with those vows, to promise for themselves if they chose to do so. Next Sunday, they would stand up and affirm the vows which others had made for them, long ago.

"But only if we mean it," the blond girl said, glaring at the freckle-faced boy.

John turned quickly to hide his smile, walked quietly

out of the room and went upstairs to the sanctuary. There he looked over the empty pews, remembered the people in them that morning, and asked God's blessing for each one.

"There are many things I don't understand," he thought. "But You understand all things. Next Sunday, when these seven youngsters stand to affirm their faith in You, in Christ as Lord, let Your Holy Spirit seek out each heart in this church and fill it." He smiled his wry smile at the tall cross above the altar, and added, "even Aunt Grace," before he went out and across the backyard, to catch the end of whatever game was playing.

Alex and Kate lived through the week after Nan's triumph—or disaster, depending on the point of view—by not mentioning it at all, except for a brief exchange on Monday, when Alex came out of his office to find her alone beside the mailboxes.

"Kate, she's worse than Simon ever was, and I have to live with it! She claims she has six months for fanatical delight, before coming back to earth. That, mixed with Simon finally falling in love—"

"Simon fell in love years ago, he just didn't admit it to himself," Kate said, smiling at him over the notice she was reading.

"That may be, but the combination of Simon the lover and that other jazz is more than a sane man can stand. Marry me tomorrow, and let Nan go live with Simon?"

"I doubt they'd be content without benefit of clergy," she said.

"True, we'll make it a double wedding." He took a step toward her and sighed, said he wished she'd step into his inner office. She refused, saying she had a class, which was true.

"One of these days," he threatened, and the vocal music teacher, coming into the room, looked from one to the other and smiled, and stored that look in his mind to discuss fully with the other teachers in the lounge.

Saturday arrived, and with it, Walter. Kate met him as she walked downtown that morning.

"I don't know why I've come home this soon after vacation," he admitted cheerfully. "I just felt as though I should. I prayed about it, and it still seemed important, so here I am. Mother will think I've flipped, but I brought the week's dirty clothes as an excuse."

"Is that your suitcase?"

He glanced at the denim bag, flopped on the sidewalk beside his feet, and said it was. "Easier to pack," he explained. "I hitched this morning and caught a ride in the first five minutes, straight to Bentley Falls. That's never happened before, Kate. The Lord must want me here."

"Without a doubt, He does," she said drily, and he laughed and said she would see, one day.

"Doesn't do to be so cynical, you that young and all," he said, swinging the bag over his shoulder. "You'll see."

When Alex came to the house that same Saturday afternoon, to take Kate riding, he found her sitting at the kitchen table, dressed in her oldest jeans and jacket, staring at a letter."

"I'm ready," she said, in a faraway voice. "I really am—"

"You have the look of someone just smashed on the head." He lifted her face and kissed her, causing a quick smile that disappeared as she held the letter up.

"From Beth. My roommate," she explained, when he looked puzzled. "I've mentioned her before, Alex, you remember. She's—well, I just don't believe it, that's all."

"Pregnant? Not unlikely. Didn't he come home last summer?"

"No, not pregnant. But filled, all the same."

"God forbid, another one?" He sat on the edge of the table, smiling. This one, he didn't have to live with.

"The Holy Spirit invaded Vietnam," Kate said. "Her husband received the Baptism there."

"Don't worry, it'll never get closer than fourth, out there."

"Fourth?" Kate was confused.

"Behind drugs, sex, and booze," he said. "Don't forget, I was there."

"I know." She sat looking at him, savoring the miracle that was Alex here rather than Alex still across the sea, and then she remembered the letter again. "That's only part of it," she said. "He went looking for Spirit-filled Christians when he came home, and found them all right, and now Beth has received, too."

"Look, honey, it isn't that tragic. As long as they keep it to themselves." He grinned, ruefully. "Not that they ever do. But at least, this pair is too far away to bother us."

"You forget the mailman, through snow and sleet and all that—Beth has sent a special message. Says this has never happened to her before, but all through Sunday's service— she's a Methodist, Alex—she kept thinking she must tell me. 'Tell Kate, tell Kate,' kept running through her mind, and so she has."

"I'll play your straight man." Alex moved around the table and stood looking out the window, frowning. "Tell Kate what?"

"The text that morning. The same one, Alex." Tears flooded her eyes, and she brushed them away with the back of her hand. "The one the Weatherhead woman sent, about finding grace to help in time of need. Hebrews 4:16."

There was a terrible, endless time of silence before Alex exploded.

"Hell!" He whirled around, his fist hit the table with a crash. "Look! This is stupid nonsense—it's got to be! It's a wild coincidence, three messages essentially the same, but from three different sources. But Kate, *it is a coincidence!* You believe that, don't you? The Lord doesn't go around sending messages like that. If He needs you, He'll damn well tell you so Himself, right? Let's go riding. I've reserved those horses—"

"I know. I'm ready, but Alex—I feel peculiar."

"I'm not surprised." He leaned with both palms flat on the table, glaring at her. "Look here, do you believe in God the Father Almighty?"

"Yes," she said, meeting his eyes. "I do."

"And do you believe in Jesus Christ, His son, as your Lord? That's a tough one, Kate. Be careful."

She stared into his eyes—something was there besides anger, she thought. A hope? Did he hope she would say yes, or did he hope for a denial? It didn't matter. Brought to this point, it was impossible to arrange an answer, even for Alex.

"Yes, I do. I know it, Alex. If He isn't Lord, He was a madman, saying all those wild things about Himself. And if He isn't Lord, a lot of wise people have been wrong a lot of years. I don't think they were." She shook her head slightly, but her eyes stared into his. "Yes, I can call Jesus Lord, Alex."

"Then that's settled. Now, unless you believe in a very limited God, He can reach you on horseback as easily as here, if He happens to need you. Let's go riding."

The first snow fell that night, and on Sunday morning, the Bishop arrived at the church, stamping his feet, as John came down to his office after early communion. They met in the hall, and the Bishop's voice bounced off the walls as he greeted John, said he was sorry he'd not come earlier, he'd meant to.

"But Grace has an amazing cook, had her for years," he said. "I couldn't refuse that breakfast."

As they entered the office, however, he dropped his voice and clapped John's shoulder. "God bless you, John, you've had a bad time of it, I'm afraid. I sent you into a nest of disorder."

"Not really." Smiling, John hung his surplice in the closet and opened the outer door, motioning the Bishop into the winter sunshine. "Maggie will have coffee ready. It will settle that breakfast," he said. "But don't slip on the ice."

They successfully negotiated the snowy, slippery path— the Bishop said he was glad he didn't wait to drive down this morning, the roads were wicked—and John led the way into the dining room.

"The truth of the matter is this," he said, pouring two cups of coffee. "Ninety percent of the church members don't know or care about Grace being angry or the charismatic group."

"Sometimes even apathy has its uses," the Bishop said. "Let me tell you about your sins." He proceeded to give a close account of all Grace had told him. He interrupted this to greet Kate and Margaret, and closed it after the first cup of coffee, when Nora and Pete came in to say good morning.

"And you," he said to Nora. "You are in trouble too, young lady. I understand, John, that you allow this girl to indulge in superstition and fantasy, and that this allowing makes you unfit to be a priest." He winked at Nora and added "Witchcraft!" in a horrible voice.

The Thorne family stared at the Bishop. John's mind whirled back to the afternoon with Grace, and then Pete laughed.

"I told you, brat, it was bound to happen. The men in white will come this afternoon. The world has learned about your birds."

Mrs. Wyndham's words came back to John. He understood them and gave a shout of laughter. But Nora was on the edge of tears.

"Th-they were only for fun," she stammered in her distress. "I only d-did them for something to do, and they're getting dirty anyhow. I meant to take them down and put up some Christmas things. I—"

"Don't take them down until I've had a look. I've never seen six hundred cranes in one room," the Bishop said.

"Seven hundred and thirty one," she answered, her poise returning as she realized he'd been teasing. He stopped midway of a sip of coffee to raise his eyebrows, ask if she'd folded every one herself.

"Yes, every one," she said.

"In that case, I hope you have received at least part of your wishes, Nora. That's a lot of paper folding."

"I have, truly I have. I have lots of friends in Bentley Falls now, and that was what I wanted, most of all."

"The Lord be praised," he said, and with another wink for her he added, "The cranes be praised also, of course."

But when the men were alone again, he told John that he was not under-rating Mrs. Wyndham.

"Nor making fun of her," he said. "Her anger is quite justified, in her own mind. She really is afraid of the tongue-speakers, afraid for the reputation of her church and especially afraid because of Walter, although she keeps insisting that with him it's just another stage. After talking to him last night, however, I wonder."

"I hope he'll be in this stage for the rest of his life," John said. "But you sent me here to—"

"I suggested you might like to come here," the Bishop corrected, gently. "I suggested they consider you."

"Certainly. You suggested." John's eyes twinkled as the older man sedately stirred two teaspoonfuls of sugar into another cup of coffee. "You did this because you thought me capable of coasting between both factions and keeping the peace. But when I look at the congregation on Sunday mornings and see the glowing, joyous faces, those are the ones who spent Friday night praying." He looked out at the stone church, turned back, and said the Bishop knew he exaggerated, of course?

"Many of the non-charismatic people are joyous in their coming, are happy in their faith and come because of it. But there is a difference, all the same. You'll see it too. The pleasantly contented ones have a wonderful knowledge of their faith in their heads. The truly joyous ones have it in their hearts." John glanced at his watch and said it was time to go, if the Bishop wanted to wash up—

"There is one thing, however," he added, as they walked back along the icy path. "How long will it last? When will this bright and shining faith become dulled by everyday use, and they all become like the rest of the congregation? How long?" His sad smile grew sadder. "Will their children inherit their faith, or will it die away?"

"But they cannot inherit." The Bishop's hand rested on John's shoulder. "They can't inherit it, neither through their genes, nor their parents' words, or from us. We try, but it doesn't work. The struggling church is proof of that. Each child must come to God himself. I heard a Pentecostal minister speak along that line in St. Louis, John. I told you there was great interest in the charismatic movement; someone invited him to talk to us, and he said it like this: 'God has no grandchildren.' "

The Bishop stepped through the office doorway and opened his suitcase, shook out his cassock. "God has no grandchildren," he repeated. "Think about that, John."

John remembered those words as the service of confirmation began, when the young people left the front row and came to the altar in their white dresses and dark suits, shoes shining and hair combed. These are children of God, not grandchildren. They come by their own faith, not by mine, he thought. Not their parents' faith or Camilla's, but their own. At least, I hope they do. In a few moments they will be newly confirmed members of the visible Body of Christ, and go down to the parlors for the reception, to drink cold punch and be kissed by innumerable ladies, have their hands shaken by the men, and will they be different then?

He presented the class to the Bishop and stepped back. It was the custom in Christ Church for the Bishop to run the confirmation service, and as John watched that rotund figure, listened to the booming voice asking the questions, he was glad.

The Bishop prayed for each member of the class, laying his hands on each head in turn. Then, standing behind the altar rail, his silver hair gleaming in the light from the window high over his head, he prayed for all of them.

"Grant you be strengthened and filled by the Spirit of God," he concluded, "and may Christ live in your hearts, by faith."

Silence, then, as the service called for silence. It was so printed in the bulletin. Silence—broken swiftly and completely by the seven kneeling at the altar rail. John was aware of his own head jerking up, of the Bishop's startled face, Camilla leaning forward in the front row. Of the choir members, eyes round, staring.

Each member of the new class was praying softly, aloud. And each spoke in a strange and different tongue.

Chapter Twenty-Two

DIVERS TONGUES—they were indeed that, John thought. He raised a hand and brushed as though they were gnats and could be brushed away. Like gnats, the sounds remained.

The freckle-faced boy stared at the cross, his eyes round and startled, as his tongue twisted around unfamiliar combinations of vowels. Blue eyes sparkling, the blond girl stuttered in her excitement, laughter behind her words. Tommy looked straight at the Bishop. Each face changed from amazed expression to joy, to peace—yes, John thought, watching, to peace.

The Bishop shattered the moment.

Raising both arms in a dramatic gesture, using his fullest, most bishop-like tones, he led the congregation in an unscheduled Lord's Prayer, and these familiar words reached down, slowly, into the seven, and gradually they joined in.

At the Amen, the silence was blessed indeed. John nodded, and the organist hurried into the closing hymn—tumbled headlong would be more accurate. She raced through the introduction, and the class returned to the front pew.

During the recessional, John stopped and quickly told Camilla to bring the class to the office. Surely, he thought, following the choir again, someone must come and explain this event. If God filled these children in this way, He would send someone to explain. It didn't occur to him that he could do it, himself, or that the Bishop might.

Kate sat stolidly in the second pew as the people followed the choir out and down the broad steps to the church parlors. *It was too damn much—Lord, how could You? Why did You do that awful thing, right in the service, right in front of everyone? Damn, oh damn!*

She bit her lips together, and checked the tears.

Lord, listen Lord, if You think for a minute that now is that time, the place where You need me, You are out of Your skull. That's a fact. Kate's hands flew upward, covered her face at this thought. She couldn't do anything, she couldn't help—if only Alex were here! She pushed her fingers against her eyelids, and he was. He slid into the pew, took her hands away from her face, gently, and held them in his own.

"What happened up there?" He nodded at the altar, but Kate was busy looking at him, thanking God for him, and didn't hear.

"I thought you wouldn't come today," she said.

"I thought so, too." He studied her face as though he'd never really examined her before. "You have good bones, know that? I woke up this morning and thought about that."

"My bones?" Kate raised her left eyebrow; her dimple appeared.

"No, not your bones, that was just a stray thought, but interesting." He chuckled. "I thought about you, and I had to face the absolutely inescapable fact that no matter what happens, I love you." He touched her cheek with a fingertip, gently. "I love you," he repeated.

Kate turned her hands over, clasped fingers with him, and smiled. She felt the pressure behind her eyes ease, the need to cry disappear. Safety was here, in these strong fingers. She wondered what the people, still moving about the back of the church, thought, seeing them sitting here, together. Mrs. Bennett, of the Altar Guild, was already putting a dust cover on the lectern. It was obvious what she thought, from her grin. But Kate didn't care. Whatever anyone thought was all right, Alex was here. Together they might be able to help her father—she sighed and asked if he'd heard, where he was sitting. If he knew what happened.

"No, that's what I asked you a moment ago. I was halfway back, and near as I could figure, the Bishop decided to run the show at the end—was that the problem?"

"Not exactly. He was busy saving the show— Doesn't he have a lovely covering kind of voice?"

"If you mean loud, yes indeed. What happened?"

"Promise not to get up-tight?"

"Might I?" His brow went up in teasing imitation of hers. "I promise," he said.

"Then—" she told him. He listened, and when she finished, he exploded, but this time with laughter.

"It's too much," he gasped, resting his head on the back of the next pew, his shoulders shaking. "Somebody up there hates this church, or loves it too much, God knows which. Or hates me—no, it couldn't be that. He sent me you." He sobered quickly. "What should we be doing? Is the Bishop fer it or agin it? Can we help?"

"I don't know, but let's go down," she said. "Dad must need moral support if nothing else, by now."

The Blanshards arrived first, in Mr. Thorne's office. "Praise God," Chris said, laughing and clapping her hands when she saw the young people. Simon came, bringing Walter with him. Camilla was there, of course.

"The Bible said it would happen. What's the fuss?" Tommy shrugged his thin shoulders and grinned. "Neat, wasn't it?"

"It sure felt funny."

"Can we do it again, ever?"

Camilla told them they could do it again, of course, whenever they wanted to. "And the special thing is that you know this morning was only a beginning. A new beginning, and with the help of the Holy Spirit, you can grow strong in the Lord." She invited them all to come after school on Tuesday and talk about it, and pray together the same wonderful way.

"Then let's get some punch," one said, and Tommy gleefully told them his uncle promised him a five-dollar bill, and he'd better get out to the parlor and collect. John watched as they rushed down the hall, a clatter of new shoes on the tiled floor. As the class trooped in the parlor door, Grace Wyndham came out.

Isobel came too, tugging at Grace's sleeve, excitedly talking. Grace shrugged her off. Feet hitting the floor in solid, tramping steps, she came toward John. He saw Isobel, still by the door, twisting her hands together, and he thought that Grace couldn't have heard the children

herself, she sat too far back. Isobel told her, no doubt—
God bless Isobel.

"Now you see!" Grace brushed past John and spoke to
the Bishop, her face marked with the usual red splotches of
anger, her eyes narrow slits in her fat cheeks. "You thought
I exaggerated! Well! It must be obvious now what happens
when a weak, inefficient fool tries to lead a church, when
fanatics are permitted to teach our children!"

"These children were not drunken as you suppose," the
Bishop misquoted, with a wide smile. He patted her
shoulder, told her to calm down. "Anger won't help,
Grace—"

"Joke!" She interrupted with a sneer. "How dare you
joke about it, these poor innocent children, led to a frenzy
by these wicked people." She turned on the Blanshards and
Simon, completely ignored Walter, who stood beside them,
and told in short explicit words exactly how she felt about
charisma, and speaking in tongues, and their own heathen
souls.

Both the Bishop and John tried to interrupt, but too
gently. She would not stop until Walter stepped suddenly
forward, grabbed her by both arms and shook her.

"Stop it! That was the most real service of confirmation
this church has ever seen! Don't you understand what
happened? Didn't you feel the Spirit there, couldn't you
hear the sign—"

"Walter, remove your hands." Her voice came in a thin,
iced whisper. "This fool of a minister has let it go on, after I
warned him. I warned him!" She faced John. "I suppose you
will do something now? This emotional frenzy is the result
of your permissiveness, your lack of leadership, your—"

"Mother! You can't talk that way to Mr. Thorne. The
Bishop will tell you it was all right, it was good."

She turned on Walter, then. "You—a Wyndham!" Her voice shook. "How dare you do this to me?"

Mother and son stared at each other, while the others watched. Then John stepped forward, too late. Grace lifted a fat hand and slapped Walter hard, across the face.

"Your hair isn't enough, or your Bible reading, praying for me! Now you take their side against me— How dare you call yourself my son?"

Simon said later it was almost visible, the anger leaping from Grace to Walter. He reared back, struck the wall and leaned against it, breathing hard. Then, while they watched, he drew in strength. His head lifted, the mark of his mother's hand faded, and he smiled. The warm blue of his eyes met the ice blue of hers.

"I dare because I am your son, mother. But I wouldn't disgrace you for the world. If you don't want me around, that's all right. I'll get my things and be gone before you get home." His eyes crinkled, suddenly, and he gave a short and joyous laugh. "Just the same, you can't stop me loving you, and better yet, you can't stop God loving you!"

He turned quickly and raced for the door.

Grace stood as though paralyzed for a long moment, looking after Walter, before she turned to the others.

"He won't really leave, of course," she told them, her chins quavering. "He is going through this stage, but he wouldn't really leave me."

The Bishop cleared his throat, Camilla patted her shoulder, but no one found words until they heard the screech of tires as Walter drove out of the lot.

"He's taking the car!" Grace looked wildly around. It was doubtful that she remembered the cause of her anger, now. "He wouldn't really leave," she said again, "but I must hurry home. You will excuse me, Bishop? You realize, of course, this is just a stage in Walter's life. He'll grow up eventually, you know. I really must go—"

She stumbled in the doorway, and Alex caught her arm.

"We'll take you home, Mrs. Wyndham. Of course it's a stage. He'll be there waiting for you, I'm sure. You'll be all right again."

Grace shoved him out of the way.

"It's just down the street, and I'm perfectly capable," she said. "But I must hurry."

Alex said yes, of course, her coat, however—and followed her down the hall. Kate turned to her father.

"Don't worry," she said. "We'll take her home. You'd better get out to your people. They're having a party out there, believe it or not."

"Impossible." John smiled, and stood outside the office watching as Kate followed Alex and Grace down the hall. Then he turned to the office again, lifting his shoulders in a helpless gesture. There must be something right to say at this moment—Christ Church offers a fine variety of entertainment on Sunday, wait until you see the second act.

But the Bishop was talking with Simon and the others—there was nothing he needed to say.

"Mrs. Frey believes that Walter and Grace will be all right," the Bishop said, when John came up to them.

"I think so, too."

"In that case, we'd better go to the party. I imagine there will be questions from those who heard."

"The understatement of the day, sir," Simon said, and stood aside, letting the Bishop lead Camilla down the hallway. John followed them all, walking slowly, wondering what came next in this unusual act of God. It would be difficult, but it could be good—he was sure of this. He remembered he'd turned the problem over to the Lord, and he thought his prayer had been more than answered.

Or just begun to be answered?

He paused inside the parlor door. Martin, dressed in his dark Sunday suit, pipe in his mouth, stood surveying the congregation as they drank coffee and talked together.

Larry Spencer captured Craig, a few steps further on. "Too much talk," he said, and eased Craig toward the doorway. "Now I saw a crack up near the Ascension window, be a terrible thing if the glass would go. As a member of the building committee, I think you should check it, too. Something has to be done."

As they passed John, Craig looked over Larry's head and winked. It wasn't the crack in the wall that Larry wanted to check, John thought.

On his right, Isobel dipped punch for the children, and Leah passed out cookies, talking at the same time.

"It's a judgment, Aunt Grace said, you heard her say that. A judgment on this church, she said, for having those awful meetings here."

Isobel gave out another cup of punch, and hugged Leah. "Of course it's a judgment," she answered. "A glorious one."

"A glorious judgment?" Leah held the plate toward John. Her dark eyes were hopeful. "A glorious one—could it be that, Mr. Thorne?"

"Why not?" John took a cookie and Leah turned away, her cheeks flushed with excitement.

"Why not?" she echoed.

Martin shifted his pipe and looked down at John. "Everything went fine, didn't it? A nice, quiet service all around," he said.

Chapter Twenty-Three

THEY HURRIED across the backyard and bundled Mrs. Wyndham between them on the front seat of Kate's car, while she mumbled about this stage Walter was going through. They did understand, didn't they, that it was only a stage? He was a nice child, and of course he wouldn't leave her. Kate reassured her, and patted the white gloves that covered fat fingers and the rings.

Alex turned at the green light on the corner by the church, and they saw, far down the empty, Sunday street, a man running. And then another. When they turned at last into the drive between the tall hedges, several people were rushing across the snow-covered lawn, and Grace screamed.

She pushed back against Kate, until Alex stopped the car and helped her out. They ran, and they found Walter.

He'd braked too late and too hard on the icy drive, at the right angle leading to the carriage house. The car had

obviously skidded into the house, bounced and flipped—
My God, Alex swore, under his breath—how fast was that
fool going? Walter lay in the snow, his shoulders against the
broken boxwood by the corner. Blood poured from his
head, streamed down his face, into his beard, onto his shirt.
His arm was strangely bent beneath him.

"May's already called the ambulance, Grace. He'll be all
right." A tall man grabbed her arm, held her as she stared at
her son.

"I've killed my baby," she whispered.

Kate said that was nonsense. "He isn't dead," she said.

Grace fell toward Walter, and the neighbor grabbed
her, said, "Don't move him. They always say don't move
them."

Sinking down beside Walter, Kate reached through the
blood with her fingers. She felt the gash on his forehead and
looked up, shocked, at Alex. The cut was wide and deep.

"I've killed my baby," Mrs. Wyndham sobbed above
her, and Kate screamed.

"Stop that! He isn't dead!" Tears came down her own
face. Walter's skin was gray, not like real skin at all. She
looked up at Mrs. Wyndham and told her to ask forgiveness, if she was to blame.

"But he can't hear me . . ."

"Then ask God! That's what Walter would do." Kate's
face matched Walter's; her body trembled. She stared at
the blood still rushing through her fingers and wondered
wildly what to do, how to stop it? She'd taken First Aid
once, but she didn't remember— If she just pressed the
edges together? She had to stop the blood somehow, or he
would die—he would surely die.

Whimpering above her head—Kate looked up. "If you
were lying here, Walter would pray." She spoke harshly.
"Get down here and pray like you never did before. Help

me!" She closed her eyes. Mrs. Wyndham crumpled down beside her and kept on sobbing.

"Lord God in heaven, help me!" Kate heard a voice saying those words clearly—her own voice. "Walter loves You and trusts You. Please, Lord—heal him!" She prayed on, in a clear but quiet voice, vaguely aware of Alex beside her, holding her. She prayed and remembered the boy on campus the summer before, the deliriously happy boy who'd prayed for her. She saw his wistful expression the day he said he was "new in the Lord."

Her voice broke at that, and she lifted her face and tried again. "Lord, in the name of Jesus, please help Walter. Tell me what to say; show me what to do."

"Alex, help me! I don't know what to do, and we must—someone must do something—"

"They're coming, sweetheart." His arm was tight around her now, holding her while she held Walter, held his head together, blood on her fingers, running into her sleeves. "Just keep praying," he said.

"Oh, please, in the name of Jesus—Walter loves Him so—save him Lord, heal him!" Her eyes looked up to the bleak winter sky. "Give me the right words, Lord," she begged, and dropped her face again, asked that he be healed, that God save His loving child, but this time the words changed.

These sounds were not her words. Kate heard a language she did not know—words that meant nothing came from her lips. Not graceful words, she thought. They had a harsh tone, yet a cleansing one. She knew they were right. They were sounds of praise and of healing, words of love, and as she listened she felt a sense of assurance, a warmth of certainty crept through her body and she was singing inside, she was singing. "Surely goodness and mercy—oh, thank You, Lord, thank You!

"Thank You, thank You—" she whispered this; the other, different sounds stopped.

Walter moved his head.

He moved his head and pulled a little away from her and opened his eyes. He looked at Kate, at his mother crouched in the muddy snow, her eyes shut tight, sobbing still, and he smiled.

"I told you, Kate," he said, his voice unsteady and soft. "I told you the Lord wanted me home for something special."

Kate, relief and the last moments hitting her at once, wiped her fingers across his cheek and said, "With a Lord like that, you've got troubles, friend."

A neighbor held out a warm damp cloth, and Kate used it to wipe the blood from his face, from around the gash in his head. She wiped it, and then wiped again, her eyes wide.

"Alex?" He bent over, and looked close. And looked again. A thin red line marked the place.

After a moment, he found his voice. "Walter, with a Lord like that, you don't need anyone else. The damn thing has closed up. If I hadn't *seen* it—"

"Praise God," said Walter, and pulled his arm from under him, flexed it gently, and smiled. Then he touched his mother's face. "Hey," he said, "look here. I'm all right. Stop bawling." Her tears came faster, her shoulders shook harder.

The ambulance slid to a noisy stop in the drive behind Kate's car, and Walter said he didn't need them, thanks just the same. At that, his mother took charge. She stopped crying and said he would certainly go to the hospital, on the stretcher. He might be full of broken bones inside.

"Yes, ma'am," he said, and cheerfully submitted. Grace climbed into the ambulance beside him, mud and snow clinging to her skirt. As the wide doors shut, they heard him apologizing.

"Sorry I wrecked the T-bird, mother," he said, and they heard the wail as Grace again began to cry.

The neighbors drifted away in small, chattering groups, aware only that Walter had been unconscious and was now awake, had seemed terribly hurt but perhaps was not. "That kid," one man said, grinning with relief. "Walter could fall in a sewer and come out smelling like a rose. I'd have sworn he killed himself this time, but he was always lucky. Smart-aleck, lucky kid."

Shoving his hands in his pockets, he took another turn around the crumpled car before he went away, whistling.

Alex walked around the car, too, came back and sat beside Kate in the snow.

"Not a total loss," he announced. "If he'd worn his seat belt, he might have been all right. Corner of the house is a mess, though."

"Alex, stop it." Her fingers touched his arm gently. "What happened couldn't have happened, could it?"

"Of course not. And not just his head, I'd have sworn the rest of him was broken sixteen ways. However—it happened, Kate."

"I know. I felt it happen, Alex. I feel it now, in my fingers."

He held her close. "If Simon were here, he'd say the Lord used you today, Kate."

She remembered the words from Hebrews, and turned a shaky smile toward Alex.

"I didn't find grace to help in time of need, it found me." She giggled, a strained and tired sound. "I never did go boldly to the throne, Alex."

"Whatever the hell that means."

Kate caught her breath, sat still in the circle of his arms. "Listen. What happened—that wasn't the Baptism, Alex. I don't understand, but don't worry, please, that wasn't—" she stopped. She'd prayed in the Spirit, in the name of Jesus, and God's answer came at once—charisma, a gift from God, to heal Walter's broken body. She wouldn't change that, no matter what it meant to herself, or to Alex.

"It's all right, Kate," he whispered, his cheek against her hair. "Remember I told you this morning—years ago, that seems—I love you."

"You prayed for Walter, too. I know you did."

"Naturally; it was the only game in town." He smiled at her dirty face, and wiped at the streaks with his handkerchief, finally gave that up and kissed her gently, and carried her to the car.

"Simon was right, after all," he said, holding her close. "What will he say, when I admit I was wrong?"

"That's easy." Joy overflowed into laughter; she hugged him. "Simon will say, 'Praise God!' "